Zenaide Alexeievna Ragozin

Siegfried, the Hero of the North,

and Beowulf, the Hero of the Anglo-Saxons

Zenaide Alexeievna Ragozin

Siegfried, the Hero of the North,
and Beowulf, the Hero of the Anglo-Saxons

ISBN/EAN: 9783337213961

Printed in Europe, USA, Canada, Australia, Japan

Cover: Foto ©Andreas Hilbeck / pixelio.de

More available books at **www.hansebooks.com**

SIEGFRIED

The Hero of the North

AND

BEOWULF

The Hero of the Anglo-Saxons

BY

ZENAÏDE A. RAGOZIN

Member of the Royal Asiatic Society of Great Britain and
Ireland ; of the American Oriental Society, etc.
Author of " Chaldea," " Vedic India," etc.

ILLUSTRATED BY GEORGE T. TOBIN

Sixth Impression

G. P. PUTNAM'S SONS
NEW YORK & LONDON
The Knickerbocker Press
1903

The Knickerbocker Press, New York

PREFACE

A STRANGE thing happened last winter in New York, strange even for New York. It was reported, with the names and addresses, in all the papers ; and personal investigation proved the facts to be true.

It happened in the family of a respectable and well-to-do German artisan couple. Both husband and wife had come from the old country very young, and prospered, as honest industry will, when coupled with intelligence and a moderate share of luck. They had profited, perhaps to an exceptional degree, by the educational advantages which Germany provides for her poorest children ; but, unfortunately, their minds and their moral sense ran in a groove. They loved truth above all things, but truth in a narrow, absolute sense. They read in their leisure hours, but only what was literally true. All fiction, all poetry was tabooed, branded uncompromisingly as "lies," and abominated accordingly. In a word, the worthy couple were specimens of a very rare genus : human beings utterly devoid of imagination.

Strictly on these lines they brought up their little daughter, a pretty, blue-eyed fairy of a child, their idol and their joy. They would give to her a first-class education. They could afford it, for their savings-bank account kept growing and had reached the sum of $1400.00. But the parents—the mother especially—watched her studies and recreations keenly, and so successfully that little Gertrude at twelve years of age had never heard a fairy-tale, never seen a story-book or a Mother Goose picture, and had never suspected that there were any other intellectual meadows to browse on than mathematics, spelling, and geography.

Now, by a perversity in which fate delights, this sober, truth-telling couple had brought into the world a being from another sphere—imaginative, dreamy, ardent-souled, artistic. Cherished as she was, little Gertrude could not be anything but happy, nor was she conscious of any unsatisfied want. But she threw her whole unconscious passion into music and showed such talent as to delight her elders and inspire them with the proudest hopes for her future career.

One day she heard her mother say to a neighbour: "Gertrude shall be another Paderewsky. She shall play at the White House before the President. What a fortune she will make!" The child said nothing, but began to think. "I was so glad," she said afterwards; "I thought it had already happened." Soon after, she went with her parents to the dedication of Grant's tomb. It was the first pageant she had ever witnessed, and she saw the President in his landau. She heard that he and his wife were staying at the Windsor.

Three days later Gertrude, returning from school, burst into the family room with an astounding piece of news: Mrs.

McKinley had visited her school, had heard her play and recite, and would return next day with the President. Gertrude was to visit them at their hotel. Great was the parents' joy. The day following, the little girl was equipped from head to foot with new garments and sent off on her supposed visit. She came home at seven o'clock in an ecstasy of joy : "Mrs. McKinley will adopt me. I am to call her 'mamma.' She will pay for my music lessons. And Mr. McKinley will give papa a place in Washington." They believed it all. But Gertrude had something else to tell, and came out with it the next day: " Poor Mrs. McKinley has no money ; she does not want to ask her husband till pay-day. I wish I could lend it her."

The father went to the bank and returned with a hundred dollars, which he gave to Gertrude to take at once to " Mamma McKinley." Very soon she was back: " Mamma McKinley thanks you ever so much. She would come to see you, but of course she cannot come to a tenement." Whereupon, incredible as it may seem, the good people moved to an "apartment" in a good location and proportionately high as to rent.

Gertrude hastened to inform her illustrious friends of the change, and came home with another woful tale : " Mr. McKinley asks papa to lend him a hundred dollars until he goes back to Washington. He has cheques, but does not like to pay his hotel bills in cheques." The hundred dollars went. This time the child came home with an armful of costly flowers. The President had sent the roses, his wife the lilies of the valley, and the violets came from the German Ambassador.

After this Gertrude became a regular visitor at the President's, but almost every time she had to have money, to lend either to him, or to his wife, or to spend in largesses to the servants, in presents to the secretaries or attendants, and each time she returned laden with flowers and even stranger gifts, which she distributed to the members of her family ; there were, among other things, a black-and-tan dog, a canary bird, and, later on, jewelry, even to a diamond ring.   At the same time the child conversed on all current political topics as one who got her information at headquarters, and gave so many and positive particulars about the position in store for her father, the salary, the work, etc., that the poor man actually returned work he had contracted for, to take a short rest before the 1st of December, on which day the summons to Washington was to come.

The $1400.00 were gone.   But where was the harm, since they would be repaid with interest, not to speak of a $5000.00 salary !

Then the crash came.

On Thanksgiving Day, Gertrude prepared to go to school, as usual.   " Is your school open to-day ? " asked her father, wonderingly.   " It is always open for the President," she replied, promptly enough, still not without a little gasp at her blunder. " I will go with you," said the father, quietly. It had just dawned on him for the first time that there was something queer somewhere.   The schoolhouse was locked, of course. She did not yet lose heart. " Mrs. McKinley must have come and gone away disappointed. I 'll run over to the hotel." " I'll go with you," again said the father, who had taken her to the door more than once. But this time he questioned the janitor. He learned that the President had left in April, that the little girl who came in at one door used to walk through the hall and out at another door.

How the good man got home, he never knew. Gertrude broke down completely and made a full confession. All the time she was away from home she spent at a neighbour's. She had a drawer there where she kept the money she did not spend and all the things she did not take home. She made presents lavishly, took her friend on long drives, but could not account for the enormous sum she had squandered. The neighbour sent home to her parents a variety of articles she had kept in storage for the child. It was a queer collection : there were, among other things, two bicycles, a camera, plaster casts of musicians, and—to the mother's great-

nothing can ever take the place of the universal treasury of nursery fairy tales, the ever young, the ever dear,—harmless owing to the glaring extravagance of their impossibilities, educational from the moral purity and profound wisdom which pervade them.[1]

Fortunately we have, ready to our hand, for the next age—say from ten to sixteen—another vast treasury of fiction, which to the same qualities adds high literary worth, besides historical value, as the source from which all the poetry, drama, romance of the world have flowed through all but unnumbered ages—the mytho-heroical epic fiction of the ancient nations. Once we admit the necessity of recreative fiction-reading for the young, why not plunge into this treasure and bring out its pearls and rubies in generous handfuls, and pour them into our children's laps to make them rich

---

[1] This cannot be said of such works as Jules Verne's famous books. Their semi-scientific plausibility is a snare to the young mind, which does not possess sufficient knowledge to discriminate between the truth and the fiction they contain, so that all its ideas get misled, confused, and blurred. A lie in the garb of truth! Can anything be more pernicious?

for life with the heirloom which is theirs by right of birth?

There are two reasons why a well selected and carefully adapted course of high-class poetic fiction must rank before the host of modern story-books—well meant and well done as many of them are—which crowd the Christmas counters: First, the positive standard value of such literature, —the noble beauty it breathes; the high lessons of unselfish heroic endeavour which pervade it, and which it instils without ever pointing a moral; the gallery of masterly characters which impress themselves on the mind forever by a few simple strokes; the vivid presentation of the life, manners, and spirit, in bygone ages, of the different peoples, with the universally human element never absent or distorted. Second, all study of history, with many of its attendant branches, is based, according to the modern methods of comparative research and reconstruction, on that of the myths and heroic legends of the ancient world. In becoming familiar with them for pleasure and amusement, therefore, the youthful mind will be storing up the materials for future serious work,—nay, when the college days come, it will find much of the work actually done.

Not that these ideas are new at all. They have been propounded and acted upon a hundred times. To them we owe such admirable gems as Hawthorne's and Kingsley's tales of the Greek gods and heroes and, while on a lower plane, Church's attractive selections from Homer, Virgil, and Herodotus, not to speak of numberless other attempts in the same field. Aye, there's the trouble : it *is* always the same field, the everlasting so-called " classic " field, while we have long ago discovered that it is but one of many, quite as rich in sterling treasure, quite as attractive with brilliant and fragrant, if exotic, flowers. Truly, these Græco-Roman stories seem worn pretty threadbare by overmuch handling, while the vast mine of the East and the North has been left either hardly touched or quite untouched. Surely there is more than room on the book-market for a series embracing the

Northern and Oriental epics.   To repre-
sent the North we have the Anglo-Saxon
Beowulf, the Swedish *Frithjof*, the German *Lay of the Nibelungs*, the Franco-Ger-
man *Lay of Roland*, the Finnic *Kalewala*,
—all of them national epics.   In the East
we have the two great epics of India, the
Mahâbhârata and the *Râmâyana*, and that
of Persia, the *Shah-Nameh* ("Book of
Kings").   The Slavic race indeed has no
rounded, finished literary epic poem, its
leisure having been broken in upon by the
inexorable demands of an iron age, which
compelled it, in self-defence, to go about
its practical historical work.   But the materials are there in bewildering abundance,
in the form of separate blocks of legends,
grouped around an heroic central figure,
as those of the Round Table around British Arthur.   Of these blocks, moreover,
chips enough have flown off, in the form
of popular folk-tales and fairy tales, to yield
a fascinating little volume of the kind of
Grimm's *Hausmärchen*.

And now about the treatment of the
national poems.

It should be simple and epical ; faithfully following the main lines, bringing out also the characteristic details,—the poetical beauties, picturesque traits, and original dialogue, as much as may be consistent with necessary condensation and, frequently, with elimination. It should be a consecutive, lively narrative, with the necessary elucidating explanations incorporated in the text and with the fewest and briefest possible footnotes, while it should contain absolutely no critical or mythological digressions. For, should such digressions be indulged in, the work would bear to the epic in hand the same relation as, say, Keightley's *Græco-Roman Mythology* to the *Iliad* and *Odyssey*.

Let me with a single example be a little more explicit.

The " Lay of the Nibelungs " (" Das Nibelungenlied ") would necessarily be one of the most important contributions to such a series as is here planned. It is the national epic of Germany, and has not yet been presented in this manner. Yet the names of the chief actors — Siegfried,

Kriemhilde, Brunhilde, Hagen—and the principal incidents of the poem have within the last few years (mainly owing to Wagner's tetralogy of operas), become as familiar as those of Homer's heroes, so that, at first sight, a new treatment of what is seemingly the same subject may appear superfluous, in view of the considerable group of books treating of Northern myths which has lately been put on the market. But all, or nearly all, of these books were written with an especial view to the themes of Wagner's operas, which takes from them scholarly authority and lowers them to the level of mere books of the play. Meanwhile the great story of the epic has not been re-told.

To make the matter clear by a parallel hypothetic case : take the whole mass of myth and tradition which makes up the bulk of Hellenic mythology, heroic and legendary history, the heroes and kings representing the later transformations of the gods. Suppose now that a great modern genius had thoroughly mastered the immense material and written a series of operas on themes taken from it,—a trilogy on the fates of the doomed House of the Atridæ, a tragic opera on the adventures of Perseus and Andromeda, etc. The operas become very popular and—the fashion, but they are too erudite to be generally intelligible. Then there come men who tell the stories of these myths and heroic legends with the special object of making the operas intelligible and the subjects of them familiar. The result is a sort of course of classic mythology, not told spontaneously and methodically, not similar—let us say again—to a text-book mythology, but biassed and bent to the main object of popularising the operas— a running commentary on them—at the same time showing the connection and transformation between the older (divine-mythical) and the later (heroic-mythical) cycles, and bringing in the interpretative methods of modern comparative mythology. Useful and instructive work of its kind. But where, in all this, are the Iliad and Odyssey?

This work has been well and amply

done with the myths and heroic legends of the North. But where, in it all, is the " Lay of the Nibelungs "—a complete, rounded piece of literary art, in itself a gallery of characters, working out a perfect plot in a series of well conceived and finely rendered situations? What we want, in telling it to the young, is to take the epic just as it is, condensing and expurgating, but not changing; rendering the characters, scenes, situations with the faithfulness and reverence due to the masterpiece of a race; using, as much as possible, especially in the dialogue, the words of the original. Whether Siegfried is the young smith of the Edda, and Brunhilde is the Valkyrie, Odin's daughter, and Hagen a reflection of Loki, and whether the whole is the myth of Sun, Earth, and Winter, preserved in the various nursery tales of the Sleeping Beauty —all these things we have no business with at all.

This, of course, is the way to treat the Eastern epics as well; to which we would add a few of the Hindu dramas, such as

Kalidâsa's *Sakuntala* and *Urvasî*, the stories of which could be told after the manner of the Lambs' *Tales from Shakespeare*.

This series being intended as parallel reading to history and planned to illustrate history, it might very properly include standard historical novels, ancient and mediæval, duly condensed and adapted ; such works as Felix Dahn's *A Fight for Rome* ("Ein Kampf um Rom"), some of Ebers's Egyptian and Roman stories, Flaubert's *Salammbo*, Gautier's *Le Roman de la Momie*, and even English romances like *Zenobia*, Reade's *Cloister and Hearth*, Bulwer's *Last of the Barons*, and others. Of course, there are great difficulties in the way, none so great as in handling such a book as *Salammbo*, Flaubert's Carthaginian novel, for youthful reading—that marvellous work of gorgeous imagination and scholarly reconstruction. At first sight, it seems impossible to fit it for young readers without disfiguring it ; yet it can be done. The book has been read aloud, with the necessary cuts, to classes of girls,

with the best results, both as to amusement and instruction. It requires some
tact and lightness of touch, together with
great reverence for your subject, entering
into the spirit of it thoroughly, and work
—that 's all.

A word now on the language. It should
be simple, though not untinged with quaint-
ness, and even in places a certain degree
of archaïsm, bearing in mind, above all,
Kingsley's strictures on "long words"
(words of five syllables he wants fined).
This does not exclude the use of what
may be called good literary words, *i. e.*,
words not in use in commonplace conver-
sation but quite at home in good literature,
especially if they belong to the Anglo-
Saxon side of the language. It is no matter that such words may sound at first
unfamiliar to young readers ; they cannot
too soon be made familiar, for it is so
much done towards the comprehension of
the higher class of literature ; and besides,
we cannot begin too soon to enrich the
young people's vocabulary, the poverty of
which, even among persons of average

culture, is among the most distressing re-sults of a mere public-school education.

But great changes are coming over the schools as well as over other branches of public life ; changes in the right direction, which may shortly amount to a revolution, when there will be no reason why these *Tales of the Heroic Ages* should not, although addressed to young people at large, find a place, if not in the school curriculum, at least in the wide margin of so-called "Supplementary Reading." It is with this expectation that each of the tales will be followed by a brief historical and critical notice for the especial use of public-school teachers and instructors generally.

May they prove acceptable, not alone to the young, to whom they are specially addressed, but also, as has been felicitously said, to "the old with young tastes"!

Z. A. RAGOZIN.

ORANGE, N. J.,
     June, 1898.

CONTENTS

SIEGFRIED

Contents

BEOWULF

ILLUSTRATIONS

SIEGFRIED

THE HERO OF THE NORTH

AND

KRIEMHILDE'S GREAT REVENGE

" The Lay of the Nibelungs"

" Das Nibelungenlied "

I

SIEGFRIED'S BOYHOOD AND YOUTH

ONCE upon a time, there lived in the Netherlands, in Xante, a mighty castle by the River Rhine, a powerful king and queen, Siegmund and Sieglinde. Far and wide spread their fame, but it was as nothing to that which their glorious son, the hero Siegfried, won. Even as a boy and beardless youth, he performed deeds of might, such and so many that his name became familiar in all the German lands. Of his early adventures, two were so wonderful that they made him immortal in song and story for all times.

Of these adventures, one was the slaying, in single combat, of a dreadful monster known as the "Dragon of the Linden-Tree," because he made his home in the thick foliage of a huge linden, these trees often growing in Germany to almost as great a size and age as the lordly oak. All the country around was kept in dread by the fierce and murderous "Linden-Dragon." But nobody was brave enough to go into the forest and fight him. So young Siegfried did his people a great service by his daring in seeking out the Dragon and killing him; and it was no wonder they praised him and loved him, and boasted of him to their neighbours. But he was to reap some good for himself too from his brave deed. He noticed that wherever the Dragon's blood had touched his flesh the skin had become hard and unfeeling. So he bathed his whole body in the blood, face and all, and became as though coated with a thin casing of horn, which made him invulnerable,—that is, not to be hurt by the cut or thrust of any weapon whatever.

Young Siegfried's other adventure brought him even greater glory, besides such wealth and power as never were man's before or after him; yet, in the end,

—in far remote later days and through many strange happenings,—it was also to bring sorrow and destruction on himself and many brave men, both true and false.

Siegfried loved to ride out alone, hunting, or simply to see the world, and take any chance to display his great strength and daring. Once, when he had ridden farther than usual, he found himself in the land of the Nibelungs, where lived wizards, and giants, and dwarfs, and things were generally queer and uncanny. When Siegfried arrived, the old king had just died, and he found the king's two sons quarrelling over the division of his treasure. It was an ancient and a mighty hoard; not a hundred farm waggons could have carried all the gold and jewels. And it had this wonderful property: that no matter how much was taken from it, the hoard never grew less. But a curse had been laid on it in olden times, that it should work nought but harm to whomsoever was the owner of it. Wherefore the old Nibelung king had had it hid away from sight and use in a deep mount-

ain cave. Now it had been brought
forth, and lay spread out in glittering
heaps before the two heirs and their
knights. They haggled and wrangled,
and could not come to an understanding. So when Siegfried suddenly stood
before them, they were glad, and asked
him to divide the treasure between them;
and, to show how thankful they would be,
they at once presented him with their
father's own good sword, named Balmung.
But Siegfried, try as he would, could not
get them to agree, they were so greedy
and unreasonable; and when he spoke to
them sternly, they grew angry, and their
people began to threaten him. Then
Siegfried's blood was up. Grasping his
new prize, Balmung, he attacked that
armed band single-handed.

Now there was magic power in the
sword, which had been forged in olden
times by a wizard with many a strong
spell. And magic work it did in the
young hero's hand, laying low twelve
chosen knights and many of the Nibelung men, and lastly the two young kings

themselves. After that the warriors were cowed into submission, and gave up to Siegfried the treasure and the whole country, with all its castles. Only the faithful dwarf, Alberich, still fought furiously, bent on avenging his young masters. It was like a mouse fighting a great lion, and would have been laughable but for the poor dwarf's devotion, which made him forgetful of his own life. Siegfried admired him heartily, and not only spared him, but asked him if he would not like to take service with himself. The dwarf replied that, now his masters were dead, there was no hero he would as lief serve as Siegfried, for none was worthier. Then Siegfried, after binding him with many strong oaths, made him his Keeper of the Hoard, which was forthwith taken back to the cave in the mountain. Alberich wore the famous *tarn-cape*—the cloak which makes the wearer invisible—and Siegfried took it from him and carried it home, together with the good sword Balmung, as proud trophies of his ride into the land of the Nibelungs. Ah me, little he thought what grievous harm was to come of that fateful ride!

At length young Siegfried arrived at the age of manhood, when noble youths are wont to be solemnly girded with the sword and to take their place among the warrior worthies of their country. Then King Siegmund sent forth heralds through his own lands and those of his neighbour kings, to give notice of the great festival to be held at his court, and to invite all the high-born youths of the same age as Siegfried to come and receive the sword of manhood together with him. Four hundred young heroes prepared to answer the King's call. And many a fair maiden and grave matron bent for many a day over loom and broidering-frame, that the youths might bear themselves bravely at feast and dance in richest robes and mantles glittering with cunning work in gold and flashing with gems. Their fathers saw to their steeds and armour, and never had so gallant a troop gathered to do honour to so young a prince.

Seven days there was high feasting, and

there were knightly games and tournaments, that the young warriors might display their grace and prowess ; and gifts and
praise were showered on winners and losers
alike, for all did well.   And the memory
of Siegfried's knighting lived long in the
land.

II

SIEGFRIED GOES A-WOOING

ABOUT this time it came to pass that a rumour reached the Netherlands, of the most beauteous royal maid Kriemhilde, only sister of the three wealthy kings of Burgundy, the brothers Gunther, Gernot, and young Giselher. So wondrous fair was she said to be, that not a month went by but some noble or princely suitor rode to Worms on the Rhine, to ask her in marriage of her brothers, the kings. But each and all rode away disappointed, for the right suitor had not come yet, and Kriemhilde would not wed unless she loved.

Siegfried grew thoughtful as he listened to the tales of the lady's beauty and her pride, till one day he declared to his father,

"This maiden I will wed, or none." King Siegmund was sorely grieved and tried hard to make him change his mind, "for," he said, "both Gunther and his brother Gernot are haughty men; I have known them long. And so are their knights, and first among them Hagen, fiercest and haughtiest of them all. I fear me much that evil may come of this wooing."

"What's the odds?" Siegfried replied. "If I may not win the maid in kindness, my strong right arm shall help me to my bride, aye, and to her brothers' lands."

"Nay, speak not so," King Siegmund warned; "for should such words be carried across the Rhine, never shouldst thou ride into King Gunther's land. The maiden is not to be had by force. But if thou must e'en take thine own way, I will send to all our friends, that they may provide thee with a seemly following."

"Not so!" cried Siegfried; "I will do my wooing myself. Twelve knights, no more, twelve trusty comrades, I will take. These, father, give me, and thy blessing."

Tearfully, and sore oppressed at heart.

the King and Queen bade their dear son Godspeed.   But he comforted them with words of loving cheer :

" Ye shall not weep for me, nor fear for my life.   Good tidings shall ye hear, of how we did you honour in the land of the Burgundians."

On the seventh morning of their journey the little band rode into Worms by the Rhine.   All silk and gold their raiment, silk and gold their horses' bridles and breast-gear ; their burnished shields and helmets flashing in the sun, their long swords clanking against their spurs,—thus they made their entrance into King Gunther's city.   All the folks ran out into the streets to gaze at them.

Soon they were met by knights and squires from the palace, who bade them welcome to their master's land and courteously offered to relieve them of their shields and take their chargers' bridles. But Siegfried curtly bade them let the horses stand and not carry away the shields, but take word to the King that a strange knight would fain have speech of him.

King Gunther was even now standing with his most trusted peers at a window of his palace, and looking out on the noble guests, as they stood by their steeds, watchful and observant. Not one of the Burgundians could tell who they were or from what country, except only Hagen, Lord of Tronje, the wise and crafty; he at once knew Siegfried, though he had never seen him, by his matchless beauty and right royal mien. He told of the battle with the Dragon and the adventure with the Nibelungs, and gave it as his advice that the young hero should be received well and honourably, and great care taken not to provoke him to anger.

"We will go down to meet him," said the King.

"You may well do that," said Hagen, "for he comes of a noble race, and is the son of a powerful king. And, from his looks, methinks it is no idle errand which brings him to us. "

Then King Gunther, his brothers, and his peers went down into the palace yard where Siegfried stood on guard, and greeted him most courteously.

"Whence, noble Siegfried, came you to our land?" the royal host kindly asked, "and what seek you here at Worms by the Rhine?"

"That," spoke the guest, "shall not be kept from you. I have heard it said in my father's land, that at your court were found the boldest champions ever king won for his own : that is what brings me hither. And of yourself I hear great praise for manly worth ; folks say no king so brave was ever seen in all these lands. I cannot rest until I find out the truth. I, too, am bold and brave, and am, some day, to wear a crown. Fain would I have men say of me that I am fit to rule—my life and honour on the venture. Therefore, if so be you are all that rumour tells, I challenge you to combat, my inheritance against your land and castles."

The King was dumb with wonder, and so were all his men—it was so strange and unforeseen. But the knights began to show signs of anger and could hardly be held back while Gunther and Gernot spoke mild and reasonable words, wishing

to turn Siegfried's perverse mood.   But
the Lord Ortewein, of Metz, the King's
marshal and Hagen's nephew, spoiled all
by a rash and insulting speech, which met
with a quick retort, when there were calls
to arms and the uproar became so violent
that Gernot's sternest command did not
for a while avail to lay it.

"No rashness, on your lives!" he cried,
when he at last gained a hearing. "The
noble Siegfried has done us no wrong as
yet, nor will he do us any, I feel sure ; we
shall, I trust, win him for our friend yet."

"Most princely hero," said young Giselher, King Gunther's youngest brother,
gentle and winsome in looks and manner,
now speaking for the first time, "you shall
be our right welcome guest ; so shall your
trusty comrades. We would gladly serve
you in all things, my friends and I."

And as he spoke, cupbearers appeared
and King Gunther's noblest wine was
handed around. And the royal host was
first to pledge the strangers.

"All that is ours, so you ask for it in
courtesy, shall be yours as well ; we will

share with you freely our blood and goods."

Siegfried could not but feel shamed at so much forbearance and gentleness. Besides, he thought of the fair maiden he came to woo, and, falling into a milder mood, suffered himself and his knights to be led into the palace. There they stayed week after week, and the time sped away unheeded, in feasts, athletic games, and knightly exercises. In these Siegfried showed himself skilful far beyond not only his own comrades, but the most famed champions among the Burgundians. The ladies of the court often graced the ring where the youths held their friendly contests, and when one or other would ask, "Who is the knight so noble of presence, so rich of garb?" somebody would be sure to answer, "That is young Siegfried, the hero from the Netherlands."

Siegfried was always ready for anything that was proposed, be it ride or hunt or joust; but he often fretted in his heart because he had never been thrown in the Lady Kriemhilde's way yet, and felt

too bashful to ask plainly for an introduction.

So a whole year passed away, and the
hero had as yet had no glimpse of the
maiden from whom so much joy and so
much woe were to come to him.

III

FRIENDSHIP

AND now it came to pass that strange tidings stirred men's minds in Burgundy. Messengers came with words of anger and defiance from Ludeger, King of the Saxons, and his brother Ludegast, King of the Danes. Not without trembling did they declare their errand when they were brought before King Gunther, for he was known to have a violent temper. They brought a formal challenge and declaration of war. Within twelve weeks the two kings would pitch their tents before Worms by the Rhine; let King Gunther look to his crown.

With a heavy heart the King called his friends together and asked their advice. His brother Gernot took the news lightly:

"We have our good swords," he said, "and we must all die some day. Let us then not forget what is due to our honour and give the foe a hearty welcome."

But Hagen the wary looked on the matter more soberly:

"I am sorry for this," he said. "Ludegast and Ludeger are overbearing men and very powerful. We cannot get ready in so short a time. Better call in Siegfried and tell him the news," he added, after a moment's thought.

This advice pleased Gunther greatly. He went himself to seek Siegfried, who quickly cheered him with words of comfort and friendship.

"Let not your hearts be troubled," the young hero said, "but leave the matter to me. I will engage that the foe shall never even see your country. Let them come thirty thousand strong, I will be a match for them with one thousand. That thousand you must give me of your men, since I have only twelve of my own; and let Hagen come with me, his brother Dankwart, and his nephew Ortewein; also worthy Folker, to bear the banner."

King Gunther now sent for the messengers, and thus spoke to them:

"Tell your kings to think twice before they start on this venture, or they may rue the day, unless, indeed, all my friends run away from me."

With this he dismissed them, to their great joy, with a safe-conduct and many rich gifts. And when they returned to Denmark and reported to King Ludegast how they had sped on their errand, they told him that Gunther had many a bold champion at his court. "Towering among the others," they said, "was one who stood nearest before the King; people said his name was Siegfried, the hero from the Netherlands."

Then Ludegast was sorry he had sent so rude a message. But what was done could not be undone, let him regret it ever so much, and the only sensible thing now was to hasten and strengthen the preparations. When the two kings joined forces, they found themselves at the head of forty thousand men, and they did not tarry a day on the march to Burgundy.

But Siegfried was even quicker. He had promised Gunther the enemy should not see his country, and he was as good as his word. He made such good speed with Gunther's army that he surprised the two kings before they could ride forth out of Saxony. He had the good fortune to meet King Ludegast of Denmark in the very first battle, and took him prisoner, sorely wounded, with his own hand, himself untouched, for every blow fell harmless on his broad burnished shield.

King Ludegast was taken to the rear of the Burgundian army. There Siegfried hurriedly commended him to Hagen's care, but would not tarry a moment himself for rest.

"I have much more to do before night," he cried, "so life and limb be safe. Many a maid and matron will mourn this day in Saxony."

And he rushed back into the fray, the princes of Burgundy close at his side.

The Saxons now had joined the Danes, and both stood their ground bravely, giving blow for blow. Three times Siegfried with his own twelve knights had cut his way into the Saxon ranks, and had been repulsed as many times, before they caught sight of King Ludeger and were seen by him.

But when the Saxon did perceive the hero from the Netherlands, with his matchless sword Balmung swung high above his head, he was filled with rage. The two champions rode at each other with such a furious shock that both the armies fell back, leaving the field free for them and their chosen knights. Ludeger plied his sword so well that Siegfried's horse fell under him; but it rose to its feet the next moment. Again and again the two rode at each other, and all around them spears flew, swords clashed and clanged in mortal strife. Many a shield was bent, many a helmet cleft, and knight after knight dropped headlong from the saddle. At last King Ludeger stayed his hand and called aloud to his men:

"Cease from the strife, my liegemen all! King Siegmund's son, the mighty Siegfried, is against us—it was an evil wind that blew him hither."

He commanded the banners to be lowered, and sued for peace. His prayer was granted, but Siegfried ordered him to follow him as hostage to Burgundy. Five hundred captives went with the kings. The Danes, shamed and crestfallen, returned home to Denmark.

Siegfried and Gernot sent fleet messengers to Worms with the glad tidings and to bid King Gunther prepare for their coming. There was much wondering and questioning, and the women could not hear enough of the glorious tale.

One of the messengers was secretly taken to the Lady Kriemhilde, for there was one to whom she had silently given her heart and of whom she would fain hear more, unwatched and at her ease. She asked who of all the princes and the knights had borne himself best in the great battle.

" Noble lady," answered the messenger,

"all did well; but if I may speak the whole truth, no one compared with the noble stranger from the Netherlands. What our knights achieved,—Dankwart and Hagen, and all the King's liegemen, —was but as wind to the prowess of Siegfried, King Siegmund's son. The greatest battle ever seen was fought by him against the two kings, Ludegast and Ludeger. Both were made captive by his strong hand and will rue it to the end of their days that they sought to quarrel with our kings. Never yet so many prisoners came to this country as he is bringing even now. Five hundred and more, sound of limb, and at least eighty sorely wounded, on stretchers,—that is mostly Siegfried's work. And so those who challenged us out of sheer arrogance are coming as captives to King Gunther's land."

As the Lady Kriemhilde heard the wondrous tale, she blushed rosy red, and spoke graciously to the messenger:

"Thou hast brought me joyful news, indeed. For thy guerdon I shall send thee handsome garments and ten marks in gold."

When King Gunther asked how many had fallen in the field, it was found that he had lost only sixty men, none among them of great note. In his joy he bade that the wounded be cared for by his most skilful surgeons, friends and captive foes alike. A great court festival with tournaments was announced and the term fixed six weeks from date, so all might have time for proper rest and healing, and those who so wished might go to their homes to be tended.

Then Siegfried would have taken his leave. But King Gunther prayed him most lovingly to tarry yet a while. He could not offer to reward him—his guest was too great for that; but in all friendship and honour he and his brothers showed their sense of his services, and so did their peers. Now Siegfried had not been bent in earnest on departing, for thoughts of the maiden filled his heart, and so he was fain to stay.

And Gernot, who may have guessed

what was in his inmost thoughts and what would please him best, spoke secretly to the King:

"Gunther, my dear brother, we owe the hero who has so freely done us such great service a token of regard that will make him proud before all the other knights. Let us take him to our sister. Let her, who never yet received knight in her bower, give him kindly greeting, that we may win him for our friend forever."

When the message was given young Siegfried, he was so overcome with joy that he could hardly master it enough to bear himself with proper dignity. And when he actually stood before Kriemhilde and heard her sweet voice bid him "Welcome, Lord Siegfried, noblest of knights!" he could only bow low and look with speechless longing in her lovely, blushing face. He had seen her before from a distance, when she walked from the palace to the ladies' seats to view the tournaments, with her mother, Queen Ute, and with her kinswomen and attendants, and

he had thought then that she shone forth among them as the dawn from among sad-coloured clouds. But it was a very different thing to stand before her as her special, much-honoured guest, and be allowed to touch her delicate hand. He thought that in all the years to come no summer day or May morning ever could yield him half the delight that filled him now. They made so fair a sight as they thus stood in the middle of the hall, that of all the gathered guests not one had eyes for any but the stately pair. But when the maiden, at her brother's bidding, granted the hero whom they wished to honour the sweet greeting of her lips, King Ludegast broke into the bitter words :

" To win the noble Siegfried so high a favour, many a brave man had to take death or wounds at his hands. The Lord keep him from ever again coming near the Danish lands !"

But now the ushers called out to make way for the Princess, that she might proceed to the minster, to hear high mass, and Siegfried fell back among the other guests, who followed in stately procession.

But after mass he was again bidden to attend the Princess ; and now they found the courage to have some talk together. Kriemhilde began :

" The Lord repay you, Sir Knight, for your generous service, for which my brothers and our friends will be faithfully beholden to you unto death."

Siegfried looked in the beautiful face as he replied :

" Ever will I serve them, nor lay my head down to rest unless they bid me, now and as long as I live. This will I do, Lady Kriemhilde, for the love of you."

Through all the twelve days of the great festival Siegfried was the royal maiden's chosen squire : by her side at the banquet, her partner in the dance, her knight in the games.

Meanwhile the two kings, Ludegast and Ludeger, being now well of their wounds, prayed King Gunther to name their ransom and the conditions of an honourable peace, so they might ride home and be free. It had now grown into a fixed habit with the Burgundian to take his guest's advice on every matter of any importance, so he sought out Siegfried and forthwith laid the case before him.

" Our guests," he said, "would fain depart to-morrow, and would know on what terms we are willing to let them go, and let peace be between our countries. So now, friend, advise me what to do. What they offer I will tell thee : gold, as much as five hundred mares can carry. This they deem a ransom fair and meet."

But Siegfried shook his head.

" Not so. Let the noble brothers depart in peace, so they pledge themselves not again to bear arms against thy land, and give thee their hand on it."

" So let it be," spoke the King, and parted in brotherly friendship from those who but so lately were his sworn foes.

Then once again Siegfried spoke of taking his leave, for he was a timid wooer and dared not speak the desire of his heart, lest it should be refused him. The

King was grieved; but young Giselher
well knew how to win him to stay.

"Whither," he pleaded, "whither, noble
Siegfried, would you ride away? Hear
my prayer: stay here with King Gunther
and our friends. Here are many fair ladies, and they will make you welcome, be
assured."

And once again the doughty Siegfried
spoke:

"Then let the horses stand in their
comfortable stalls, and put away the
shields. I did mean to ride home, but
young Giselher's loving-kindness holds
me, a willing bondsman."

So the hero stayed, to please his friend.
And things were so ordered that scarce a
day went by without his seeing the Lady
Kriemhilde and having speech of her.

IV

BOUND FOR ICELAND

SOON after these things had happened by the Rhine, it began to be rumoured that King Gunther was thinking of taking to himself a wife; wherefore there was great joy in Burgundy. But his mind did not incline to any of the daughters of the land.

There lived a maiden queen on an island beyond the sea ; so beautiful, yet so strange in her ways, there was no other like her in the whole wide world. She was stronger than most men and better skilled than most in warlike exercises. Few could have matched her in throwing the spear. But her favourite feat, wherein she had no equal, was this : she would hurl a heavy stone disk to a great distance and give at the same time such a mighty leap that she would land on her feet by the very spot whereon the disk had just fallen. She had published far and wide that she would wed no man but one who should win three athletic games against her. Any man was welcome to try, but if he lost, the forfeit was his head. Many a noble suitor had gone to Iceland to woo Queen Brunhilde, and had never been seen again. And the Queen was still unwedded.

One day King Gunther sat taking his ease among his friends. Somehow they came to talk about his marrying, and each had some noble maiden or other to pro-pose. The King listened for some time in silence, then suddenly declared:

"I will sail across the sea and woo Queen Brunhilde. I will chance my life on the venture, for I care not to live unless I win her for my wife."

"That I would not advise," Siegfried broke in; "the Queen is fierce of temper; the cost is too high. Cast out all thought of her, I pray."

"The woman is not born," Gunther retorted, "let her be ever so strong and bold, whom I cannot master easily, single-handed."

"Speak not of what you know nothing about," Siegfried warned again. "Four such as you could not stand against her anger. Wherefore, out of my love, I pray you, attempt not so mad a thing; let Brunhilde alone."

"Be she never so fierce and strong," spoke Gunther, now thoroughly aroused, "I go. To win so rare a creature, something may well be risked. Who can say but I may win, and she may follow us to the Rhine?"

"Then let me advise," began Hagen, who had not spoken yet, "that you beg Siegfried to share the venture with you. It is the wisest thing you can do, since he alone knows so much about Brunhilde."

The King at once turned to his guest:

"Most noble Siegfried, wilt thou help me woo and win the lady? Do so, and I will be beholden to thee forever, with love and life and honour."

Then answered Siegfried, King Siegmund's son :

" I will, so thou promisest me thy sister
as my guerdon, Kriemhilde, the fair royal
maiden.   No other meed do I desire, no
other will I take."

" I promise," spoke Gunther joyfully,
"and here is my hand on it."

The friends joined hands and swore to
stand by each other.   Then they at once
began to consult about the best way to
carry out the undertaking.   Gunther proposed to take over an army of thirty
thousand men.   But Siegfried would not
hear of it.

" Let us," he said, "do this thing after
the fashion of true knight-errantry.   We
will go, just the two of us, and two more
—Hagen, I should say, and his brother
Dankwart, brave men both,—and I will
dare any thousand men to stand in our
way."

King Gunther was greatly taken with
the idea.   And now they began forthwith
to consider the question of clothes, most
important for heroes bound on such an

errand. Gunther was for asking his lady mother to provide them with a proper wardrobe, in which they might appear with dignity and to advantage before Brunhilde and her ladies. But sly Hagen advised him to ask his sister instead ; she would know better what would be becoming and after the latest fashion ; the young understand one another best on such an occasion.

So Gunther and Siegfried sought Kriemhilde in her apartments, and the three had a long consultation, which ended in her promising to have ready twelve suits for each of the four companions,—to be worn during four days, three for each day,— such as they need not be ashamed to be seen in at Brunhilde's or any other queen's court, provided she was supplied with enough gold, silver, seed pearls, and precious stones ; of stuffs and embroidery silks she had sufficient store.

As soon as the two friends had taken their leave, Kriemhilde called to her thirty young maids, her companions, all skilled in finest needlework. They took silk

stuff of Arabia, white as snow, and velvet
green as clover, and embroidered them
lavishly with gold and many-coloured
stones. Kriemhilde cut the garments with
her own hand. They also took skins of
rarest fishes and made pouches thereof,
working them with silks, to carry gold in ;
the effect against the light-coloured garments was most striking. There was no
stint of silk stuffs from Morocco, and
from Libya too, such as only royal youths
were wont to wear ; neither did Kriemhilde
spare her own store of ermine pelts, to
provide the knights with rich and stately
mantles. In seven weeks' time the work
was done and a messenger sent to bid the
knights, who, in the meantime, had been
busy building and equipping their ship,
come and survey their new wardrobe and
try the garments on, for any alterations
that might be needed. But nothing more
perfect in fit and workmanship had ever
been seen, so everybody declared ; and
when the heroes, after giving the noble
maids due thanks in courtly words, began to
say farewell, many a tear-dimmed eye was

bent on them where they stood, so handsome and so brave. And suddenly Kriemhilde threw her arms around her brother's neck.

"Oh, dearest brother mine," she said with breaking voice, "go not from me, from thy land and thy friends! There be women enough nearer home, and nobly born, to be wooed and won without venturing life and limb."

Her tears fell fast, and dimmed the gold chain on her breast, for something in her boding heart told her darkly of the evil that was to come to them all from this fateful wooing. But quickly controlling herself, she turned to the royal guest from the Netherlands:

"Noble Siegfried, to your true and loyal care do I commend my dearest brother: keep him from harm in Brunhilde's land!"

The hero held out his hand:

"So long as breath is in me, you may, noble lady, rest free from care. I will bring him back to you unharmed, here, to the Rhine. My life on it."

Eleven days and nights the royal suitor and his three friends were carried smoothly before the wind, towards Iceland's shores. On the twelfth morning they beheld the green and prosperous isle, studded with strong castles, among which towered one, grander and more splendid than the rest, beetling almost over the water's edge.

"This," spoke Siegfried, to whom alone the land was known, "this is Isenstein, Queen Brunhilde's own residence and stronghold. Keep your wits together, so you are not dazzled with the bevy of fair women whom you will see assembled there. And hark: one word of advice before we land. When we are asked our names and errand, we will all hold to the one tale: that Gunther is my liege lord, and I am his vassal. It is best so. All this mislikes me sore," he added, when they had promised to do as he bade them; "nor would I embark on it, Gunther, merely for love of thee. But thy sister, the lovely maid, is as my life to me, my very soul, and I would fain win her for my wife."

V

GUNTHER'S WOOING

MEANWHILE the ship was nearing the strand. It passed so close under the castle that the friends could see the beautiful ladies who were crowding the windows and peering curiously at the new-comers. Siegfried pointed them out to the King.

"Take a look at them," he said, "and tell me which would be your choice at the first glance."

"I see one at yonder casement," Gunther replied quickly, "in snowy gown; she is so stately and graceful: she would be my choice if my eyes were the only umpires."

Said Siegfried:

"Your eyes have not misled you; yon

beauteous maiden is indeed Queen Brunhilde."

While they were conversing, the Queen bade the maidens retire from the windows; she deemed it unseemly for ladies to take note of the doings of strange men. But they had had time to see how the four stepped ashore, how Siegfried led forth from the ship a handsome charger, and held the bridle while Gunther mounted; not often before had the noble youth done such squire's service to living man. He soon forgot it; but Brunhilde never.

Siegfried and Gunther were both clad in spotless white; their shields silver, and milk-white their steeds, as like as though they had been twins. Hagen and Dankwart, on the contrary, were clothed in sable from head to foot, and mounted on chargers black as night.

They found the gates of the great castle, with its eighty-six towers, wide open. Brunhilde's men hastened to meet the guests as they rode into the castle yard, to take their horses and their shields. They were also requested to yield up their swords and cuirasses. Hagen at first angrily refused, but Siegfried explained that such was the law of the land, and that no guest might enter the presence of the Queen except unarmed.

When the knights had taken due rest and refreshment, they were ushered into the great reception-hall, the walls of which were cased with priceless green marble, and soon Brunhilde entered, attended by one hundred maidens in gay and rich apparel, and by five hundred of Iceland's bravest warriors, sword in hand. The sight was not pleasing to the four.

As Siegfried was the only one known to Brunhilde, she addressed her welcome to him, and of him inquired the object of their voyage.

"I thank you humbly, Lady Brunhilde," he replied, "that you deign to greet me before this noble knight ; the honour, in truth, belongs to him, for he is my liege lord. His name is Gunther, King of Burgundy by the Rhine. For love of you he has made the long voyage, for he desires to wed with you. I came

because I am his vassal, and he bade me
Else most certainly had I stayed away."

"If such be his desire," the Queen replied, "he must play against me the games
which I shall propose. If he wins the
match, I will be his wife. If he loses, the
forfeit is his life and that of all his companions. And with your lives you lose
your knightly honour as well. Therefore
pause and reflect betimes."

Siegfried quickly went up to Gunther
and whispered in his ear:

"Speak to the Queen freely and fear-
lessly, and let nothing trouble you: I
will guard you and help you out with
certain wiles known to me."

Thus encouraged, Gunther answered,
nothing daunted:

"Most noble Queen, I accept the challenge and the conditions. Life is worth-
less to me if I cannot win thee for my
wife."

Forthwith the Queen retired to arm
her for the game. Hagen and Dankwart
stood apart the while, silent and sullen.
The thought of both was, "In an evil

BRUNHILDE RECEIVES THE BURGUNDIANS.

hour we embarked on this quest"; but they would not utter it.

Siegfried meanwhile quietly slipped away and hurried to the ship, where he had left the tarn-cape—that wonderful cloak which not only makes the wearer invisible, but increases his natural strength twelvefold. When he returned to the hall, he could mix with the crowd and observe all that was done and said, himself unseen. A vast circle had been drawn, and around it pressed over seven hundred warriors, in full armour.

When Brunhilde re-entered the hall, she looked as though she were going to fight for the lands of all the kings on earth. Over her silken tunic she wore mail armour of finest golden wire. The shield that was brought her was of polished gold, but under the gold there was hard steel of great thickness. Four men carried it with effort, but she slung it with ease over her shoulder by a broad baldrick, richly worked in emeralds. Then three attendants brought her the spear which she was wont to throw, a most grim and grewsome weapon, with its double-edged head, to the making of which had gone a hundred pounds of iron.

As Gunther looked, his brow grew darker and darker. "What is all this?" he thought. "The Devil himself could not stand against her. Were I but safe and sound at home by the Rhine, long might she live and prosper, unwooed of me."

Hagen and his brother Dankwart whispered together in helpless rage. "Had we but our swords," they said, "the beautiful fiend should die before harm came to our dear lord, though we had sworn a hundred oaths to keep the peace."

Brunhilde heard them, and looked at them smilingly over her shoulder.

"Since they think themselves so mighty," she said to her attendants,— "bring them their armour, and give them back their swords. I do not care whether they are in full armour or bare to the skin. I never yet met the man whose strength I need dread. I do not think King Gunther will be the first."

Last of all the disk was brought in. It

was so large and heavy that twelve men could hardly carry it. Yet they were valiant men and strong in battle. Then a great fear came over the Burgundians: "What manner of woman is this our King would woo?" Hagen spoke out loud. "Would she were down below, the Devil's own bride!"

And now she rolled her sleeves up her snowy arms, took her stand, holding the shield with her left, and with her right swung high the spear: that was the signal to begin. Gunther shuddered at the sight. But suddenly he felt a hand touch his own, and Siegfried's voice spoke low in his ear:

"It is I, thy comrade. Have no fear whatever. Let go the shield, I will hold it. And keep in mind what I now say: make thou the motions; I will do the work. But never let the Queen know of these my wiles, or she will surely be revenged on thee."

Never had Gunther heard more welcome words. Just at this moment Brunhilde hurled the spear with such force and such perfect aim that it pierced through the centre of the shield which Siegfried held before the King, striking sparks from the steel, and both men were thrown off their feet by the shock and the weight. But for the tarn-cape they had both been surely killed.

Siegfried pulled the spear out of the shield, and thinking, " I will not slay the maiden ; it were a pity, she is so fair," turned it and hurled the shaft end against her armour, bringing her to the ground. She sprang to her feet in an instant and cried : " I thank thee, noble Gunther, for thy courtesy !" She gave him all the credit, little dreaming that she had been thrown by one far mightier than he.

She was on her mettle now, and as she took up the heavy disk, put forth all her strength. Never had she thrown it so far, or leaped so lightly, her golden armour clanging as she landed on her feet. The disk had fallen fully twenty fathoms away, and she had leaped beyond that mark. Gunther, with unseen Siegfried by his side, ran to where lay the monster stone.

He went through all the motions of weighing, balancing, and throwing it, while Siegfried performed the act. Both throw and leap left Brunhilde's mark far behind —a great wonder, when one thinks that, in leaping, he carried Gunther along. As they stood by the disk Gunther alone was seen.

Brunhilde's lovely face flushed dark with anger, for Siegfried had saved the King from death. When she saw him standing safe and sound at the very end of the circle, she turned to the crowd and spoke :

"Ye all, my friends and liegemen, step near : from henceforth ye are King Gunther's subjects."

Then all laid down their swords and did homage at the feet of Gunther, the wealthy King of Burgundy. With courtly grace he greeted them as he took their Queen's right hand.

Suddenly Siegfried appeared with most unconscious mien, and, walking up to the King, asked him why he tarried so long with the games, as it were well the matter were decided. He acted ignorance to perfection.

"What!" cried the Queen, "is it possible, Lord Siegfried, you did not see the games which King Gunther won? Where could you have been?"

Hagen, as usual, was ready with an answer:

"Our noble Siegfried had gone to look after the ship; that is why he saw nothing of the games—to his loss and our grief."

"This is joyful news indeed, fair lady," cried blunt-spoken Siegfried, "that there is an end of your overbearing ways, and that one is found fit to be your mate and master. And now, noble Queen, you will follow us to the Rhine."

He had better have left such words unspoken. Brunhilde was not one to forget them, though now she answered mildly enough:

"That may not be yet a while. I cannot leave my kingdom on such short notice. My kinsmen and vassals must be sent for first."

Messengers were sent out, and in a few

days troops of warriors, both knights and squires, well armed, well mounted, began to arrive. This made the friends somewhat uncomfortable, and Hagen, who was prudent and given to see the dark side of things, gave voice to the feeling:

"Woe is us, what have we done? Who can tell what the Queen is scheming? What if she be wroth with us?"

But Siegfried was undaunted.

"Be not troubled for so little," he said; "I will go and bring you help,—a thousand choice men. Ask me not who they are or whence they come; and when I am gone, make no sign. I shall be back before I am missed."

There was much comfort in these words. "Only," spoke the King, "stay not away too long. We may need help."

"In a very few days ye shall see me again," Siegfried assured him. "If the Queen asks for me, say you sent me on an errand."

4

VI

THE DEPARTURE

THOSE who happened to look out on the sea the next morning, at dawn, beheld a sight which made them rub their eyes in wonder and doubt: they saw a ship, with all sails set, rapidly driving before the wind, from the harbour into the open sea, without a sailor on deck or a pilot at the rudder. It was the ship of the Burgundians, and Siegfried, made invisible by his tarn-cape, was steering it. One day and night of fair weather and favourable wind brought him to the land of the Nibelungs, where the great treasure lay hidden and well guarded.

As he made fast the ship in a sheltered cove, it occurred to him to test the loyalty of his men. He walked to the castle gate and, with his features concealed by the visor of his helmet, disguising his voice, asked for admission as any wayfarer might. The warder, seeing a knight of tremendous size, in full armour, refused, and fought with all his might when the stranger broke open the gate. Sooth to say, Siegfried had to put forth his great strength to throw the man and bind him. This was good service, and he vowed in his heart he would not forget it.

The noise of the fighting had been heard in the mountains by the dwarfs who guarded the hoard, and Alberich, the keeper, hastily donning armour, came running to the castle, where he attacked Siegfried with the only weapon he could use with any effect, on account of his size : a heavy whip with golden handle and seven lashes ending in hard knobs. With this he belaboured the stranger till his shield was all out of shape. Siegfried would not hurt the faithful dwarf, so he just pulled his beard and bound him as he had bound the giant warder, then stopped to recover his breath and rest his badly bruised limbs.

"Who are you?" gasped the dwarf.
"Had I not pledged my service to the
greatest hero in the world, I would willingly serve you till I die."

Siegfried uncovered his face.

"I am Siegfried.   Methinks you might
have known me.   And now," he said as
he untied the dwarf, "run to the mountains and bring me here in shortest time
one thousand Nibelung warriors, the pick
of the host."

Three thousand came.   But Siegfried
would have no more than one thousand,
and these he equipped most gorgeously,
filling their pouches with gold and silver.
Nor did it take long to provide ships and
all necessary supplies.   Was not the treasure there which never grew less, no matter how much was taken from it?

Great was the wonder in Iceland when
a large fleet, with swelling, snowy sails, was
seen to glide along the sunlit waters, making for the harbour.

"That is my military escort," King
Gunther explained to Brunhilde; "I left
it not far from here, and now have sent

for it. See Siegfried standing on the prow of the foremost ship. I wish you to go down to meet them in the castle yard and give them courteous greeting, so they may know you are glad to see them."

And now the Burgundians began to hurry Brunhilde, for they did not feel at ease in her country and were anxious to get home. They hardly left her time to set matters in order and dispose of her treasure, her rich wardrobe, and great store of precious things. She gave away much; the rest— mostly silks, gold, and jewelry— was packed in twenty large chests and stowed on board the royal ship. Her Isle of Iceland she placed under the rule and care of her own uncle, until such time as the new lord, her husband, should send a governor of his own choice. For her escort, to match the thousand Nibelung warriors, she selected two thousand men of the best. She also took along eighty-six ladies and a hundred maidens, all young and fair, that she might have a court and attendance of her own in the strange new land.

Many tears were shed, by those who left and those who stayed, there on Iceland's rocky strand, when the hour of parting came. Full lovingly the royal maid bade farewell to her people and her country. She was to see both nevermore.

VII

BETROTHED

THE voyage was prosperous and gay, with smooth waters and gentle, favourable breezes, and there was music and singing on the ships. But on the ninth day Hagen sought Gunther and reminded him that it was high time to send off a messenger to Worms with the joyful tidings.

"Right, friend Hagen," assented the King; "and no messenger could be more welcome than yourself. Therefore hasten home at once, and tell them we are coming."

But that did not suit Hagen's plans.

"Not so, my dear lord," he replied; "I should make but a poor messenger; that is not my line. Let me be treasurer

and chamberlain.   I will remain with the
ships and look after the women's safety
and comfort.   Send Siegfried instead.
And should he refuse, then beg him for
love of your sister to do you this one
more service.   He will not say nay to
that."

It all happened as the crafty Burgundian had foreseen.   Siegfried did not like
the idea of being sent on errands like a
mere retainer ; but the name of Kriemhilde, the hope of seeing her several days
sooner, and the thought of the pleasure
his news would bring her and of the bright
looks she would give him for his pains,
overcame his pride, and he said "yes" to
all.   Then Gunther proceeded to give him
most detailed instructions :

"Tell my mother, Queen Ute, that I
am happy beyond words.   To my brothers
and all our friends say how we have prospered in this wooing.   Bid Ortewein, my
loving cousin, see that a great stand is
built by the landing-place on the Rhine,
for our friends and liegemen ; he must
send them word betimes.   And tell Kriem-

hilde I trust she will, of her sisterly kindness, receive my dear bride with all love
and courtesy, for which I shall be beholden
to her all the days of my life."

There was great wailing in Worms when
Siegfried was seen to enter the city with
four-and-twenty knights and nothing was
seen of Gunther. As they dismounted in
the castle yard, the King's brothers rushed
to meet them, and when Siegfried had laid
their fears at rest with his good news, they
at once escorted him to the Queen's apartments, where he was eagerly admitted.
Kriemhilde scarcely took the time to greet
him.

" Welcome," she said, " Lord Siegfried,
peerless knight. But tell us, where is
King Gunther, my noble brother? How
is it with him? I fear me much Brunhilde's strength overpowered him, and
now he is lost to us. Oh, woe is me, poor
maid! why was I ever born!"

Spoke Siegfried with smiling face:

" Fair ladies both, ye weep for no reason that I know. With one word I will
make you glad: he is safe of limb and

happy in mind, and I am here to tell you, with his most duteous love, that he and his bride are within a short distance of this city. He commends her to your kindness and hopes you will both meet them at the landing, whither all his friends are bidden."

Queen Ute heard the tidings with composed and dignified mien and gave thanks for them in gracious but measured words. But the maiden was too young to have her feelings under such control; the sudden passage from sorrow and fear to great joy unmanned her, and she found no words at first, but dried her streaming eyes with her snow-white robe. At last she bade the hero sit.

"I would not grudge all my gold in payment for this news," she said. "But you are too high-born for that. So I must e'en be content to pay you with poor thanks."

"Were thirty crowns mine," he cried, "I would take a gift from *your* hand."

Castle and city now vied in busy preparation. Both were thronged with guests

from as far as they could come on such
short notice. Kriemhilde bade her maids
take out of chests and closets their very
richest attire. Ermine and sable were
as plentiful as silks and velvets; shapely
waists and arms were encircled with girdles
and bracelets of gold and rarest gems.
Such, too, were the trappings of the women's palfreys. And those who saw Kriemhilde of Burgundy ride forth that day from
the castle, down to the Rhine, with her
following of nigh on two hundred ladies
and maidens, the fairest and stateliest of
the land, beheld a sight which none forgot to their dying day. Siegfried was
allowed the privilege of riding at her
bridle-rein, to do her knightly service,
while Ortewein, the Marshal of the Court,
had charge of the Queen-mother, Ute.

Many a lance was broken in play while
waiting for the ships. Then when they
approached the landing, and the warriors
from Iceland and Siegfried's Nibelungs
had landed and formed in line on the
shore, there was sky-rending shouting and
much clanking of shields as King Gunther

stepped on his own Burgundian soil, hand in hand with his hardly won Queen.

Kriemhilde was the first to come forward and meet the stranger; she greeted her with warm yet modest words; the two embraced and kissed in most sisterly fashion; then Queen Ute came up and welcomed her new daughter with a kiss upon her rosy lips. It was some time before all the greetings had been spoken, and as the three royal ladies stood alone in the middle of the wide space kept free around them, all eyes were bent on them, and all the thousands of men and women could gaze on them at their leisure. Years after, men recalled the picture they made; but while they would speak with praise of Queen Brunhilde's beauty, they would, for maidenly loveliness and delicate bloom, award the prize to their own home-grown flower, the gentle Kriemhilde.

VIII

THE WEDDING

THAT evening in the castle, before King Gunther entered the banquet-hall, Siegfried came to him and summoned him, in his usual blunt way, to redeem the pledge he had given him before they started for Iceland. The King took the reminder with smiling face :

"What you ask for is but your right. I have not forgotten the oath I swore with lip and hand. I will help you to the best of my power."

And he forthwith sent for his sister. When she came, with many fair attendants, young Giselher met her at the head of the stairs and begged her to send them away, as the King wished to speak to her alone.

They led Kriemhilde to where Gunther stood, and round him in a circle noble knights from many lands. Brunhilde was just passing, with her following, on to the banquet-hall; she stopped, to look and hear.

The King turned smilingly to those around him.

" Friends and liegemen all," he said, " will you help me entreat my sister that she may take Siegfried for her wedded lord ? "

In one voice they replied, " That were most meetly don ! "

Again the King spoke :

" Noble maiden, sister mine, I pray thee, of thy goodness and thy duty, redeem the pledge I gave. I swore that thou shouldst wed Siegfried the hero, and if thou dost take him, thou wilt do me right sisterly service."

The maid replied with seemly modesty :

" Dearest brother mine, you have not need to beg. Right willingly I will obey you and wed the man you have chosen for me ; I am in all things yours to command."

Siegfried's handsome face flushed with joy and pride as he proffered his lifelong service to the lady. She stood with downcast eyes, shy and blushing, as is maidens' wont, but he took her in his arms and gave her the kiss of betrothal before all the court.

That evening at the banquet, King Gunther sat by Brunhilde, but the place of honour was given to Siegfried and his lovely bride, and his Nibelung knights sat to the right and to the left of them. This was so sore a sight in Brunhilde's eyes that she could not hide her vexation, and tear after tear rolled down her cheek. The King quickly took alarm :

" What is the trouble, lady mine, that thus early bedews and dims my love's bright eyes ? You should laugh and be glad, for you are queen over all my broad lands, my wealthy cities and strong castles, and many thousands of brave men are waiting on your will."

" Nay, but rather should you weep," she retorted pettishly. " My heart aches for your sister, to see her sitting by a common liegeman of yours. I must weep, I cannot help myself, that she should be thus lowered."

To this King Gunther replied somewhat sternly :

" Speak not of what you do not understand. When time and leisure serve, I will explain why my sister weds Siegfried. May she live long with him in joy and peace !"

But she insisted :

" The pity of it ! Such beauty as hers, such gentleness, thrown thus away ! Had I my will, I could fly away from here. But this I tell you, my lord King : not a word will I speak to you in friendship or in wifely duty till I know the reason why Kriemhilde must be Siegfried's bride."

" Thus much," replied the King, " I may tell you even now, and you may believe my word : Siegfried is himself a king, has lands and castles as many as I have myself ; therefore, peerless as I hold my sister, I hold him her worthy mate."

But nothing that the King could say availed to dispel the gloom which had settled on Brunhilde ; she sat with lowering brow and thoughts intent on mischief.

That night, when the feast was over and the guests had gone to their rest, she kept her word and met the King's most loving attentions with the same sullen silence. In vain he pleaded for a word, a look ; all she answered was, " Not till I know what I asked you." At last the King grew angry and changed from tenderness to more masterful language. Then Brunhilde, forgetting that she was no longer the free maid of Iceland, gave way to her temper and laid violent hands on her lord. As it was not he who had conquered her, he could do nothing against her, once she chose to put forth all her strength, and she soon had him bound hand and foot with her long silk girdle, then tied him fast to a nail in the wall, and so left him for the night, ordering him, as she retired to her own room, not to disturb her rest by moaning or speaking. As for her, she slept soundly till morning.

It was quite early yet when she unbound him and bade him with surly words take a morning nap.   She did not wish to disgrace him before his court, but would not make friends with him herself.   Poor Gunther was naturally very crestfallen, and could not quite command his face; so that everybody noticed the dejected air which he wore at church, where both the newly wedded pairs went in solemn state to hear high mass, and afterwards at the royal table, and at the games which followed.

Siegfried saw it all and was much concerned.   He stole to the King's side at a moment when no one looked, and asked softly, " Is anything wrong ? "

Then Gunther told of his mishap.

" See," he ended, " see my hands, how swollen they are.   She squeezed them so, the blood almost spurted from under the nails.   I was as a child in her hands; I surely thought my end had come.   Truly," he cried, in bitterness of spirit, " I have taken to my home with this woman shame and disgrace."

" There must be an end of her pranks," Siegfried declared with determined mien.

" I will undertake to bring her to reason.
To-night, when you are escorted in state
to your apartments, I shall join the procession, but I shall wear my tarn-cape, so
no one will see me. I shall blow out the
light in the hand of one of your link-
bearers, as a token to you. You shall
have no more trouble with your wife."

"So you do not kill her," the King replied, "I care not how severely you
punish her. She is a terrible woman."

That night, just as the King and Queen
were entering their apartments, the light
suddenly went out in the hands of one of
the attendants. By that token Gunther
knew Siegfried was there. He immediately dismissed everybody and bolted the
door. There was but one light, in a distant corner of the room, and that was
shaded, so it was quite dark. And now
began a strange performance.

Siegfried approached Brunhilde and,
without saying a word, took hold of her
arms. She, thinking of course it was
Gunther, shook him off, bidding him beware how he angered her again, unless

he wanted to pass another night like the
last. Then he gradually began to put
forth more and more strength, and so did
she, and they wrestled. So evenly were
they matched that it was long before he
could gain the slightest advantage over
her. In their wrestling they upset chairs
and tables and stools, and swayed so
violently from side to side that Gunther
had more than once to run out of their
way and crouch in corners. Once Brunhilde had Siegfried pinned to the floor and
he was but just in time to snatch the
girdle out of her hand. After this he
gained steadily, for his endurance proved
greater than hers, and at last he had her
at his mercy and was just going to bind
her, when she began to plead with broken
voice :

"Noble King, forbear. Take not my
life. I will henceforth be thy dutiful wife,
nor again do aught to anger thee. I ac-
knowledge thee as my lord and master."

Then Siegfried quietly unbolted the
door and stole out, carrying away with
him Brunhilde's girdle and a little gold

ring which he had taken from her finger without her noticing it.

The next day both Gunther and Brunhilde showed happy and loving faces. She was to him ever after as kind a wife as man need have; and all might have been well, had not Siegfried, in a freak of boastful recklessness, given the girdle and ring to Kriemhilde, whom he loved more every day. A piece of thoughtlessness which was to cost many and many a brave man his life.

A fortnight longer lasted the bridal festivities. Then all the guests dispersed, well pleased with their entertainment and bearing away rich gifts. Siegfried and his lovely wife also took an affectionate leave of their friends and kinsfolk by the Rhine, and, escorted by the thousand Nibelungs, started on their way to Xante, in the Netherlands, where they were anxiously expected.

IX

THE INVITATION

TEN years flew past. Both royal households prospered and lived happy. Kriemhilde made herself greatly beloved of King Siegmund and Queen Sieglinde, and also of the people of the Netherlands. Even the wild Nibelungs became devoted to their gentle Queen. And soon after Siegfried's return to his own land, when Queen Sieglinde died, the old King solemnly made over to him the crown and government, declaring that he himself had well earned some few years of happy rest and would enjoy the freedom from the care and toil of state and war. Siegfried and Gunther never met in all these years, but their friendship was kept up by frequent kind messages and loving gifts.

And when a boy was born to each, each
named his own for his friend ; so Siegfried's boy was Gunther and Gunther's
was Siegfried.

But Brunhilde had never forgotten the
grudge she had taken upon her wedding-
day, and moreover insisted on regarding
Siegfried as her husband's vassal and subject. And so, when she had been married ten years, she began to think to
herself : "I wonder what makes Kriemhilde bear herself so arrogantly. Her
husband is nothing but a liegeman of ours,
yet he has done us no service in all these
years."

She did not speak her mind out openly,
but tried crooked ways to get round to
her ends. She began to talk to the King
of her great desire to see Kriemhilde
again, and at last asked if he would not
send for her and her husband.

"How can you talk so ?" the King replied, reprovingly. "They live too far
away ; it were too much to ask of them."

"I don't see that," she retorted ; "no
matter how powerful a vassal may be, it

is his duty to wait on his liege lord's commands."

Gunther could not but smile at his wife's overbearing manner. He wished in his heart to see Siegfried again, but duty or service had little to do with the wish. But she insisted; only now she coaxed.

" Dear my lord," she said, " if so be you still have some little love for me, do find some way to get your sister to come to visit us. You could not do anything that would give me more pleasure. She is so gentle, of such sweet and noble bearing, that the very thought of her does me good. I mind me well how we used to sit together when you and I were first married. And right noble was her choice when she took the doughty Siegfried for her lord."

She begged and pleaded till the King at last said :

" Well, then, know there are no guests I would rather see ; so you have an easy task of it when you strive to win me over. Be it so—I will send messengers to them."

So thirty knights were chosen—a goodly

embassy. They carried greetings and most loving messages from Gunther and Brunhilde, and Gernot and young Giselher, and from their mother, Queen Ute, with entreaties that Siegfried and Kriemhilde might come to Worms on a long visit, to see their affectionate relations, when a great court gathering and tournament should be held in their honour. To make the invitation still more pressing and pleasing, a kinsman of the Burgundian royal house and Siegfried's warm friend, Margrave Gere, was placed at the head of the embassy.

Siegfried had, for the last few years, been residing in Norway, the Land of the Nibelungs, being fonder of it than of the Netherlands, and thither his brother-in-law's envoys travelled to seek him. It was a long journey and took them three weeks. They were very weary when they arrived, but the welcome which they received, the rest and good cheer, soon restored their strength. It was some time before they could tell the real object of their coming, they had to answer so many

eager questions.   But when at last Margrave Gere proffered the invitation in due
form, it was joyfully accepted, one thousand Nibelung warriors volunteering to
escort their King and Queen as a guard
of honour.   Even old King Siegmund declared his intention of going with them,
taking his own following of one hundred
knights, for he wished to become person-
ally acquainted with his son's Burgundian
relatives.   Now that it was decided, they
were all impatient to get off, and when
they dismissed the envoys they promised
to follow in twelve days.

When Margrave Gere and his companions arrived at Worms, they rode
straight to the palace, and, as they dismounted, everybody ran to meet them,
deafening them with shouts of greeting
and with questions ; everybody wanted to
know how they had sped on their errand,
so that Gere had to chide : " When I have
told the King," he said, "you shall know
too," and passed on to the King's apartments.

Gunther sprang from his chair when he

saw him enter ; Brunhilde rose to greet
him.

"How fares my noble Siegfried, my
loving friend?" asked the King.

"Tell me quick, is Kriemhilde coming?" broke in the Queen. "And is her
beauty still as perfect as before she left
us?"

"Is my daughter in good health and
spirits?" Queen Ute inquired.

Gere managed to answer all these questions at once :

"They are both well. They are both
coming. And many knights with them."

Then he had to tell in detail all that be-
fel him and his companions on their journey and at Siegfried's court ; and all the
gifts were displayed which had gladdened
every one of the envoys.

"Well may he give with both hands,"
sullen Hagen was heard to mutter. "He
holds a treasure which he could never
spend, though he lived a thousand years.
Ah, would that the hoard could be brought
over here to Burgundy!"

X

THE VISIT

SIEGFRIED and Kriemhilde were so diligent in their preparations that they were ready to start at the appointed time. They had no thought but of pleasure ; never did lighter hearts speed on more fatal journey. The only thing that damped their spirits at the last moment was that they had to leave their little son behind. But he was under good and trusty care, and as he bade father and mother good-bye, he never dreamed that he was seeing the last of them for all time.

Messengers sent on betimes announced their coming. As soon as King Gunther heard that they were within a day's travel from Worms, he sought Brunhilde in her apartment, and, sitting down by her, said :

"Do you remember how my sister received you when you first came to this country? You will now, to please me, so receive Siegfried's wife as she then received my bride."

"That will I," she replied heartily, "right gladly ; to please you, and to please myself too, for I love her well."

"They will be here to-morrow morning," he went on ; "so do not loiter, that they may not come upon us unawares. It has not often been given me to welcome guests so dear."

The meeting was most joyful and affectionate. The queens, having embraced and kissed, looked at each other long, and walked away with their arms around each other, while Gernot and young Giselher took possession of Siegfried, and Gunther gave respectful greeting to the aged Siegmund, whose coming such a distance he rightly took as a great compliment. Hagen of Tronje, too, and his nephew, Marshal Ortewein of Metz, showed themselves courtly hosts — an unwonted effort for Hagen.

The guests were hardly given time to rest before the festivities began, so great was the desire to see them. The days were taken up with jousts, sham battles, and all knightly exercises; the evenings with feasting and with dancing. Again Siegfried sat in the seat of honour, with his thousand Nibelungs to the right and to the left of him. And again Brunhilde wondered that one who was her husband's liegeman should make such a display of wealth and power and bear himself so independently.

Each morning hosts and guests went in to hear high mass in peace and harmony. Gunther and Siegfried walked together to the minster, when the bells called to mass, and so did the two queens, under a canopy, surmounted with a royal crown. Then they walked out of church in the same order and proceeded to the palace and to the banquet-hall. Things went on thus peacefully and pleasantly for ten days, for Brunhilde as yet had no unkind feelings towards her guests. She only kept thinking to herself: "I cannot bear this much longer.   In some way or other I must get Kriemhilde to tell me how it is that her husband, in all these years, has neither done us any service nor paid us any tribute : for, after all, he is our vassal."

She bided her time, waiting for a chance. And the evil enemy of mankind, who is ever on the watch to do harm and mischief among men, took care to bring about the chance she looked for, though not in the way she might have wished.

XI

'THE QUARREL

IT was afternoon on the eleventh day of the visit. Tilting and lance-breaking were going on in the castle yard just before vespers, and many of the ladies, not a few men also, were looking on from the win-dows. The two queens sat together at one of them, interested and amused, when something, in an evil hour, prompted Kriemhilde to remark:

"If everybody had their deserts, all these lands should be my husband's."

"How could that be?" replied Brun-hilde. "If no one else of the family were alive but you and he, these lands might be his; but not so long as Gunther lives."

"See there!" cried Kriemhilde, point-ing down, "see where he moves about so lordly amidst knights, as the full moon amidst the paling stars! It gladdens my heart every time I see him thus."

"However lordly be your husband," Brunhilde again replied, "however handsome and stalwart, he is not the equal of Gunther, your noble brother and my lord. You must know that Gunther is greater than all the kings that live."

"Nay, so worthy is my husband," retorted Kriemhilde, waxing warm, "that what I say of him is far from idle praise. In many ways has he achieved high honours. Believe me, Brunhilde, he is fully Gunther's equal."

"Hardly that," replied Brunhilde, still good-naturedly. "You must not take it ill of me, because I am not speaking without good reason. When I first saw them both in Iceland, that time King Gunther played against me and won my hand in such heroic guise, I heard Siegfried himself call himself the King's liegeman. I heard, I say, and therefore it is I have always counted him our vassal."

"If that were so," the fair Kriemhilde

retorted, "evil had been my plight. How could my noble brothers have wooed so ill for me, as to mate me with a subject? No, no, Brunhilde, if you love me, leave such words unspoken in future."

To which the Queen made answer:

"I cannot and never will. Am I to renounce our right to every knight whose sword is pledged to our service?"

Kriemhilde now was thoroughly angered.

"You will have to renounce all claim to one, anyhow," she said, "for he will do you no service, take my word for it— never in the world. He is a hero worthier than even my brother Gunther, that blameless knight. So prithee, spare me such unseemly words. And besides, how comes it, if so be he is your liegeman and you hold such great power over us both, that he has withheld his duty from you so long? Enough of this, I say. I am sick of your overbearing ways."

"You forget yourself," said the Queen, haughtily. "Enough words, say I too. This very day shall show whether you are in truth held in as high honour as I am myself."

Then Kriemhilde spoke again, and by this time both the women were panting with rage:

"Be it so. Since you have dared to call my Siegfried your man, the knights of both the kings shall see, when I walk into the church, whether I am not entitled to take precedence of the Queen of Burgundy. I will let you see that I am nobly born and free, and that my husband is worthier far than yours. For I will not brook the slur on my own name. This very day shall you see your liegewoman walk before you in the presence of all the knights of Burgundy. I will take my stand higher than any daughter of royal blood that ever wore a crown.—Come, ye maidens, 't is vesper time; array yourselves for church. And if any one of you have some piece of rich and rare apparel that she treasured against some great occasion, let her don it now: this day shall decide whether I may stay here any longer, free from blame and shame."

Not many minutes passed before Kriemhilde descended the stairs attended by her forty-three maidens, in such rich attire as would have befitted a coronation feast. In the palace yard they found Siegfried's men awaiting them. Brunhilde, with her women, also in their bravest finery, were joined by Gunther's knights. Thus two separate processions formed and advanced towards the minster —at which the townsfolk marvelled much, as they stood gazing and agape.

The two queens met before the minster's wide-open doors. Here Brunhilde, with frowning mien, in angry tones, loudly commanded Siegfried's wife to stop. "It is not meet," she cried, "that a liege-woman should pass before the Queen."

Kriemhilde's retort came quick and bitter:

"It had been better for thee hadst thou held thy peace. But since thou wilt have it, I ask, Can she who has been a man's bondswoman ever be a queen?"

"Whom dost thou mean?" Brunhilde cried, aghast.

"I mean thee. Siegfried, my beloved husband, wrestled with thee and mastered thee, laying thee prostrate, at his mercy, on the ground. By rights, that made thee bond to him. My brother Gunther was not the man to cope with thy untamed strength. How, then, canst thou claim Siegfried for thy liegeman?"

Brunhilde was speechless with horror and amazement. She could only murmur, "I will ask Gunther," and broke into tears. When Kriemhilde, with her following, swept before her into the church, she did not attempt to hinder her. But she did not follow. She stood all through the service, outside on the porch, surrounded by her own women and knights. She did not speak a word, but kept turning thoughts of hatred and vengeance over and over in her mind.

At last the service was over, and Kriemhilde, with all her following, came out of the minster. Brunhilde met her face to face.

"Stay!" she commanded, "one moment more! I have heard words—now give me proofs."

Kriemhilde showed the little gold ring on her finger.

"This ring," she said, "Siegfried took from you and brought to me. Again I tell you, you had better let me pass."

"Oh!" cried Brunhilde, "that ring was stolen from me; I have missed it for years; now I see who was the thief!"

And she cast a withering look on Kriemhilde. But Kriemhilde had not yet done.

"You shall not call me thief," she said. "You will not hold your peace: then take the consequences. Do you see this girdle that I have here, wound around my waist? That also Siegfried brought me with the ring."

When she saw the girdle, Brunhilde broke down, and, between tears and sobs, sent for King Gunther in haste. He came at once, and asked, with great concern, what had happened to distress her so. When she had told him, he frowned heavily and sent for Siegfried.

Great was Siegfried's amazement at the scene he found. He looked from one to the other, and asked, wonderingly:

“What are the women crying for, and what is it all about?”

Gunther eyed him gravely:

“I find much serious matter here. Your wife, my sister Kriemhilde, has grievously insulted the Lady Brunhilde, my Queen: she has called her your bonds-woman before all these witnesses. Did you ever make such boast?”

“Never,” said Siegfried; “if she has said any such thing, she shall be made to rue it. And I will clear myself by oath, with hand and lip, before your whole army: I never made such boast.”

Then the Burgundians were made to stand in a circle and Siegfried stretched out his right hand. Gunther declared himself satisfied, and they parted seemingly as good friends as ever.

But the mischief was done. Siegfried could not have acted differently. For the good of all concerned he had to clear himself by oath when the matter came to the test, but he bitterly repented in his heart his weakness in letting so dread a secret out of his own keeping and in giving the ring and girdle to his bride of a day. Gunther, on the other hand, for the same reasons, had to show himself content and dismiss the whole matter lightly, as a piece of gossip between two angry women. But he knew right well that Siegfried must have told his wife, since she could not possibly have known in any other way. Still, so strong was the friendship between the two men, and so deep Gunther's sense of Siegfried's services, that even this cloud, heavy as it was, would have passed away in time, but for Brunhilde's vindictiveness and Hagen's malicious promptings.

He had sought the Queen immediately after the quarrel and vowed to avenge her on Siegfried's person. Gernot and Ortewein, the Marshal, came in also, and straightway began to devise ways of putting him to death. Only Giselher, the youngest of the three brothers and Siegfried's staunch friend always, tried to pour oil on the angry spirits:

" Alas ! my friends, why nurse such evil thoughts ? Siegfried has done nothing to deserve such hatred, nothing that should make his life forfeit. And women, we all know, will quarrel about many things."

The King himself spoke in this sense:

" He never did us aught but good. Let him live in peace. Why should I hate him? He has been our willing, loyal friend through all."

But all the others were set against Siegfried, though with no reason at all. Still no one dared to act directly against the King's command. But Hagen kept repeating to him day after day how that, if Siegfried were no more, many a land would become subject to him. Then Gunther fell into a deep, brooding melancholy; he resisted more feebly, till once he said to Hagen:

" Oh, do cast off all such murderous thoughts. He never did us harm, but always good. Besides, know you not that he is of such wondrous might, that the man is not born who could overcome him in fair combat?"

Now Hagen had Gunther where he wanted him.

" Let not that trouble you," he said reas-
suringly. " Everything shall be carefully
prepared. But Brunhilde's tears shall be
brought home to him. When he slan-
dered the Queen, he did not count on
Hagen."

"But how can the thing be done?"
Gunther asked weakly.

" Nothing can be easier. We will get
sham messengers to come to Worms,
men whom nobody knows, and they shall
make us a declaration of war. As soon
as Siegfried hears of it, he will want to
help you and offer to take the field with
you. Then we shall have an easy task.
Only there is something I must find out
first from his wife."

So persistent was the evil counsellor
that the King at last gave way, and the
two now discussed together the unholy
plan.

XII

TREASON

EVERYTHING happened as Hagen had planned. The sham messengers came, pretending to be sent by Burgundy's old foes, the kings of Saxony and Denmark, Ludeger and Ludegast.

Siegfried was noble and honest to the core, and therefore easy to deceive. He was so indignant when he was told that the two kings intended to break the peace they had solemnly sworn when he so generously obtained their release free of ransom, that he entreated Gunther to let him make this quarrel his own and fight it out with only his own men. He would not hear of Gunther stirring from Worms, only asking him to look after Kriemhilde and keep his aged father Siegmund in good health and spirits. Things could not have favoured the traitors more. Many among the King's men knew of what was going on and were ashamed, but did not dare openly to disapprove.

While Siegfried was busy looking after the horses, and arms, and supplies for his troop, Hagen went to seek Kriemhilde, as though to take his leave of her, and was received by her with cousinly kindness. She was bright and hopeful.

"I am proud to think," she said, "that I have brought into the family a man who can save my brothers so much trouble. And now, friend Hagen, I hope you remember that I have always taken pleasure in serving you where I could, and that I never in any way offended you. Let that plead for my dear husband : do not bear him any ill-feeling for what I did to Brunhilde. I have long regretted it. Besides, he has punished me so severely for having grieved the Queen, that my body has borne the marks this many a day, so she may surely be content."

"You ladies will make friends again in

a day or two," Hagen replied, lightly. "And now, Kriemhilde, dear cousin and lady mine, tell me how I may best serve Siegfried your lord, and I will do so most willingly."

"You are my kinsman," she said, "and I will confide in you. You know that when he slew the dreadful Linden-Dragon, he bathed in the monster's blood, and that made him proof against all weapons. Yet when he is away from me, I am in mortal fear, because I know there is one spot on his body where he can be wounded, and how can I say that a random spear or arrow will not hit that spot? For while the blood was spurting hot from the Dragon's wounds and he was bending down to bathe in it, a leaf from the linden-tree fluttered down and settled between his shoulders. That spot was not touched by the blood and therefore can be pierced. I will sew a little cross with fine silk on his coat just where the leaf fell, and, Hagen, dear friend, you must promise me always to be near him and cover him with your shield, so that no foeman's weapon can hit him from behind. I place my dear lord in your loyal safeguard, and thereby place in your hands more than my life. Fail me not, and you may rest assured that I will be your loving and much beholden cousin as long as we both live."

"Dear lady mine, I will do my best," was all Hagen said—and forthwith sought out Gunther, full of unholy joy :

"I know now what I went to learn. Let us dispose of those messengers and order the hunt."

Thus Siegfried's own devoted wife, out of the fulness of her love, betrayed him to his death !

Early the next morning the hero cheerily rode forth, eager to do another good service to his friends. Hagen rode behind him, so close that he could plainly see on his back the little cross in silk. Then he fell back and secretly sent off two of his men to court. They were to pretend that they came from Ludegast and Ludeger, who had changed their mind and wished to remain on friendly terms with Burgundy.

As soon as the false embassy was received, a messenger was despatched post-haste to recall Siegfried, who was inclined to grumble at having such brave sport spoiled. But he regained his temper and his spirits when Gunther proposed a great hunting expedition into the mountains of Odenwald, which teemed with bears and boars, with deer and other big game. He only staid to see his wife before they started, for they were to be away several days, perhaps weeks.

During his absence Hagen told the King what he had learned and exactly how he meant to manage. Never was blacker plot hatched by blacker soul. Gernot and Giselher refused to go; they would have no part in it. But they did not warn the hero, and so shared the guilt, and had to pay for it with the rest, in due time.

XIII

SIEGFRIED'S DEATH

WHILE Hagen and Gunther gave their orders for the chase in which nobler game than bears and boars was to be hunted down, and the pack-horses with provisions and other necessaries were starting for the forest, Siegfried was tarrying with Kriemhilde, whose heart was heavy and boded evil. He soothed her and talked to her, and many times kissed her rosy lips.

"Dear heart," he said, "why these tears? God will grant that I find thee safe and well, and keep me so for love of thee. In the meantime, while away the hours with good friends. I shall not be long gone."

But she was thinking of what she had

told Hagen, only did not dare to speak of it. And she wept and wept, and would not be comforted.

"Oh, let this hunt be," she begged. "I had such a bad dream! Two wild boars were chasing thee across the heath, and on their track the flowers were dyed red. Ah me, but I am afraid! treason may be dogging thee. One never knows whom one may have offended unawares, and hatred is watchful and dangerous. Stay here with me, dear my lord ; 't is love that bids thee."

"Why, dear one," he said, "I shall be back in a short time. I know of nobody here who could bear me hatred or envy. Thy friends are all well disposed towards me, and surely I have well earned thy brothers' love."

"Alas, my Siegfried," she still wailed, "I fear some evil thing may befall thee. And I had another dream : two mountains fell on thee in a valley, and hid thee from my sight. If thou goest from me, I shall wear myself to death."

He took her in his arms, and kissed and

petted her, then left her quickly and was gone.   But she stood long just where he left her and could not control her grief. For she bethought her of still another dream which she had dreamed years ago, long before she ever saw him.

She dreamt she had reared a falcon. It grew up handsome, strong, and wild, and she loved the bird dearly.   Then two eagles attacked it and killed it before her eyes.   Nothing ever had grieved her so. And when she awoke, she told her mother of the dream.   Queen Ute read it thus: "The falcon," she said, "is a noble lover. God pity and save him, or it will go ill with him."   She laughed lightly, and boasted she never would love or wed—as maidens will.   But now the dream came home to her; she knew her falcon had gone from her and nothing could bring him back.

Meanwhile the great chase had begun. The hunters separated in many parties, with their several packs of hounds, having first agreed on the meeting-place, where the attendants were to wait for them with tents and provisions. Soon the mountains and the forest resounded with the blast of horns and the baying of hounds on the scent. Boughs broke crackling and dry leaves rustled as the scared game rushed wildly in all directions. And when, at a signal from the King's horn, the noble hunters met at the appointed place, a beautiful grassy glade on a sunlit mountain-side, each had something to tell and something to show for his morning's work. But Siegfried cast down in the midst of the gathering a live bound bear, which he had captured with the help of his favourite dog and flung across his horse. There was much shouting and laughing at the joke; but when he cut the thongs that tied the bear's feet and snout, and the furious beast made a rush through the throng, to the rear, where the meal was cooking, upsetting attendants and kettles, scattering the fire, and scaring the horses, the laughter changed to shrieks of fright, until the bear was seen to make, on a run, for the wood, with the hounds after him in full cry. Siegfried gave him a considerable advance, then started in pursuit. Several others started with him, but soon lagged behind; there was only one man fleet of foot enough for such a race. All clapped and shouted in wonder and praise when the hero of the Netherlands, bounding up to the fleeing beast, despatched him with one thrust of the sword, then returned, calm and smiling, with breath unspent, to where his comrades stood.

It was no town-bred hunger with which the hunters sat down to the ample feast provided for them. Not less hearty was their thirst. Great, therefore, was the disappointment when it was found that this part of the refreshments had been forgotten; not one cask of wine or mead had been sent up. Gunther and Hagen alone knew that the mishap was not due to chance. Both played their parts well. Gunther chid his cousin, and Hagen excused himself by saying that the drink had, by mistake, been sent to the wrong place.

" But," he said, " I know the loveliest,

coolest spring, not far from here, at the foot of a large linden-tree. Let us go there."

And when all arose, eager for the water, he added, with wily intent :

"I have always heard it said that no one can win a race from Kriemhilde's lord, when he is in earnest. I wish we could see one ! "

"So you shall," cried Siegfried, who was in boyish spirits that day ; "let us race to the spring ! And I shall wear all my hunting-gear, while you may run in your shirts."

He quickly belted on his sword, good Balmung, took up his shield and spear and bow, and threw his quiver over his shoulder. Hagen and Gunther, instead, cast off all their clothing, except only their long white linen shirts, in which they stood side by side as the signal was given, when they started through the clover like two wild panthers. But Siegfried stood by the spring long before they arrived.

They willingly confessed themselves beaten, and he quickly threw off his quiver, leaned his spear against the linden-tree, and laid down on the grass Balmung, his shield, and the panther skin which hung down his back. Thus he stood in his tight-fitting black hunting-coat, a right royal, noble figure, beneath the wide-spreading, shady tree, by the clear, cool forest spring, and courteously signed to Gunther to drink first. The King took a long draught, and as he rose to his feet Siegfried stepped up and prepared to do likewise, looking neither to the right nor to the left. At this instant Hagen, with swift and stealthy motion, took away the bow and sword, and grasping the spear, drove it with all his strength between the hero's shoulders as he bent over the water, into the very spot marked by the little silk cross, so that his warm heart's blood spurted forth and crimsoned the murder-er's white linen shirt. He did not stop to draw out the spear, but ran—ran as never man ran before.

Siegfried bounded to his feet and reached out for his sword or bow, but, finding neither, picked up his shield and

ran in pursuit of Hagen. So great was his strength that, hurt to death as he was, he reached him, and closed with him, and battered him with the shield till it bent and nearly broke in twain, and the precious stones with which it was studded started out of their settings and rolled to the ground.

A moment more and Hagen must have fallen under the shower of mighty blows. But the wounded man's strength suddenly gave out : his cheek and lips blanched, he swayed on his feet and sank down among the wild flowers, and they were dyed red in his blood.

"Oh, ye cravens !"—he spoke with voice still strong and clear—" is this the reward for all my love and service ? This day's work will shame many yet unborn, and as for you, the living, it parts you from the company of all good men forever !"

The knights crowded around him where he lay ; to many this was an accursed day. Whoever knows what honour is, and truth, has wept for him.

The King of the Burgundians also bent

over him, and began to wail and lament.
But the dying man chid him bitterly :

" Where is the sense of the doer bewailing his own deed? Better have left it undone."

Hagen also chid the King in his own brutal way :

" I know not what you should regret. Let us rather rejoice that we are rid of his excessive might. For there are not many left now who could stand up against us."

The dying hero heard, and once again he spoke :

" You may well boast, as things have turned out. Had I but suspected the murderous blackness of your heart, you should have little to boast of. Yet nothing in the world grieves my soul, but only the thought of Kriemhilde, my wife. She is your sister, Gunther : let that plead for her. And if you are still capable of loyalty to any human being, let me commend my dearest love to your pity and favour."

He paused, and stirred uneasily in cruel pain ; then, with his last breath, came, low and broken, the prophetic words :

"The time is coming when you shall rue this day's work. Believe me, I speak the truth; in dealing death to me, ye have dealt it to yourselves."

The breath had fled, and still the flowers drank the flowing blood.

There was a long silence. Then they laid him on his golden shield, and began to consult in whispers what they should say, so it might not become known that Hagen had done the deed. They agreed upon a tale of Siegfried having ridden off too far into the forest alone, and having been attacked by outlaws. But Hagen would not have it so.

"I shall take him home myself," he said. "I care no whit if she hears the truth, she who could so cruelly wound our Queen's feelings. Whether she weeps or not, or whatever she does, matters very little to me."

XIV

SIEGFRIED'S FUNERAL

THEY waited till the evening, then turned towards home and recrossed the Rhine. Never was more disastrous hunt. For the game that was slain that day many a woman's tears were yet to flow.

Hagen seemed possessed with a fiend of wickedness and revenge. He had the dead hero taken quietly to the palace and laid before Kriemhilde's own door.

By daybreak the cathedral bells began to ring, and Kriemhilde, who never missed early mass, waked her maidens, and called for a light. The chamberlain who brought it stumbled against the body, saw the red, blood-soaked clothing, and, without pausing to look who it was, rushed into Kriemhilde's presence, crying :

"Lady, stay within! there is a knight lying dead before your door."

Her heart misgave her at once. In a flash she thought of what she had told Hagen, and she knew the worst. She sank to the floor without a word, in a faint; but when she was aroused, she gave a cry so piercing, it was heard through the palace.

Her attendants kept repeating, "It may be a stranger."

"No," she replied, "it is Siegfried, my beloved lord. Brunhilde planned the deed, and Hagen did it."

She bade them take her where the hero lay. She raised his head with her own white hand.

"Oh, woe is me!" she cried, "that thou shouldst fall, not in the noble fray, but by a vile assassin's hand! Let me but know the doer, and my whole life shall be given to avenge thee."

Loud and bitterly the Queen's attendants wept and wailed with her. But she sent some to call Siegfried's men, and others to wake King Siegmund.

The aged King would not at first believe the tidings and chid the messengers for making sport of him. They bade him listen, and he would hear the women's wailing. Then, trembling and dazed, he hastened to Kriemhilde's room, followed by all the Nibelungs. He took his dead son in his arms, and cried over and over again, "Oh! accursed journey! accursed land!" So loud was the wailing of this great crowd, that not only the palace resounded with it, but the castle, and all Worms, the city by the Rhine. And the warriors from Nibelung swore a great oath: to avenge him at any time or place. Then they hurried away to arm themselves as for war.

But Kriemhilde would not let them do anything rash. She feared they all might meet death at the hands of her brothers' men. She rushed about among the naked, uplifted swords, begging and commanding, reasoning and restraining. At last she appealed to Siegmund's authority.

"My lord King," she said, "keep them back till we know more. My husband

shall be avenged, and I will help you.
Only let me have proofs, and the doer
shall get his deserts some time. But let
me advise you not to seek a quarrel, for
the people here by the Rhine are fierce
and violent, and there would be thirty of
them to every one of you. Stay here in
the house with me, and help me mourn
and bury my dead; that is our first duty."

Siegmund and the warriors answered:
"Dear lady, it shall be as you will."

All that day noble knights and ladies,
and citizens of note, came pouring to the
palace, to view the hero on his bier. All
mourned with the widow, and were sincere in their words of sorrow, for no one
had ever seen Siegfried but did love him,
and no one could think what the city's
favourite had done, to forfeit his life at the
hands of his nearest and dearest. And
many a plain burgher's good wife wept
with the Queen and her ladies.

The next morning, at daybreak, Kriemhilde had her dead love borne to the minster, there to lie in state, in his coffin
of gold and silver, bound with strong

steel, to the knell of all the bells in the city, and the funeral chanting of countless priests and monks ; when, lo ! King Gunther joined her with his following. Grim Hagen too was with him, who should, for very shame, have stayed away.

"Dear sister," began the King, "I am sorely grieved at thy great sorrow. I would give much could this be undone. We all must ever mourn Siegfried's death."

" You have no cause," she replied, coldly, "or this would not have befallen. You never thought of me when you took my husband from me. Would you had taken me instead !"

Gunther persisted in denying that he had any share in Siegfried's death. But Kriemhilde spoke aloud so as to be heard by all :

"Those who protest their innocence may prove it very easily : only let them approach the bier, here before the people. The truth will be manifest at once."

It is a wonder often beheld that when the slayer approaches him whom he has slain, the wounds will bleed afresh.   And this was seen by all, that time Hagen stood by the bier : the ruddy blood began to flow as freely as when the wound was made.   A shout of horror went up to the minster's roof.   But Gunther still denied.

"Hear me," he cried ;—"hear the truth. He was killed by outlaws.   Hagen never did it."

"I know these outlaws well," she replied ; "Gunther and Hagen, you it was who did it—and may God requite you as you deserve !"

At the word, Siegfried's men would have rushed on the Burgundians ; but Kriemhilde once more restrained them. And just then her two other brothers came, Gernot and young Giselher ; they grieved from their hearts for the dead and for their sister, and she received their kindness willingly, for she did not suspect that they had known of the plot, and now, in sooth, they were sorrowful enough ; the blinding tears stood in their eyes.   They spoke to her words of brotherly comfort and cheer.

But comfort nor cheer could reach the aching heart.   Only, when the funeral mass was sung, and the lid was fastened on the coffin, she ordered her chamberlains to give from Siegfried's store, with full hands, to all that came. For three days they gave and gave ; and many that came poor—beggars, widows, orphans— went home rich for many a day to come. Monasteries, too, and churches were lavishly remembered, and more than a hundred masses were read in those days for the departed hero's soul.

On the third morning, not only the cathedral but the vast churchyard around it was crowded to overflowing with sorrowing men and weeping women.   As men lifted the coffin to carry it to the grave, the loving, faithful wife was so overcome that she fell to the ground as one stricken unto death.   They poured water on her from the well, but so long without effect that many wondered that she came back to life at all ; and when she did at last, and found the coffin gone, she rushed to the grave into which they were about to lower it, and clung to it and cried :

"Oh ye, my Siegfried's liegemen, one boon I crave of your merciful hearts, one little boon in all my endless misery; let me look but once again, for one brief moment, on his beautiful face !"

She begged so long and movingly that not the hardest heart could have withstood her.   So the strongly welded coffin was broken open, and the Queen was led to it.   As she raised the comely head and kissed the brow and lips, a great wonder was seen : her eyes shed tears of blood. A miserable parting !   She was borne thence, a fair, unconscious burden.   All that day and night she passed from one fainting fit into another, and nothing that anybody spoke reached her dull and deadened senses, nor did any food or drink so much as touch her lips.

XV

KRIEMHILDE'S WIDOWHOOD

OLD King Siegmund was very ill; almost as broken by his great sorrow as was Kriemhilde herself. His first words, when he could rouse himself to think and act, were, "We will ride home. This is no place for us." He never doubted but that Kriemhilde would go with him, and such was at first her intention. But her mother, Queen Ute, and her favourite brother, young Giselher, besought her not to return to a country where, Siegfried being dead, she would be among strangers. Gernot came and also begged her to stay. They promised her that she should never be forced to meet Hagen or anyone whom she held to be her foe, that they would care for her and make good her loss as far as they could by their loving kindness.

So when King Siegmund came to her again and begged her to make haste, as all was ready and he was loath to tarry another hour among the Burgundians, she said, sadly but firmly:

"My lord King, I cannot go with you. I have no kindred of my blood in your country, while here, whatever betide, there are at least a few who will help me mourn."

King Siegmund was sorely grieved and tried to move her from her resolve.

"Not so," he said; "you shall wear the crown and our friends will hold you in as high honour as when Siegfried lived. And, daughter, think of your son: would you have him grow up an orphan with a living mother? Return to him; he will comfort you, and all our liegemen shall serve you with their swords."

But she was not to be moved.

"Go," she said, "in the Lord's good keeping. You shall be well escorted. As to my boy, I commend him to your care and to the love of all your noble friends."

When Siegfried's Nibelungs were told

that they would have to return without their Queen, they raised a wail as for another dead. Both they and Siegmund knew it was a parting for all time, and as he kissed her cheek, the tears ran down his own. But she was stern and cold, and seemed glad when they left her to herself and to her grief. She even sent all her women home. But among Siegfried's friends there was one who refused to leave her: it was Margrave Eckewart. He stayed, with his own men, and swore to serve her unto death.

Young Giselher escorted the King and his men all the way to the Netherlands, then returned to Worms—and Kriemhilde always said that no one ever gave her any comfort in her grief save only her boy brother, he was so good and true. As to Brunhilde, what did *she* care whether Kriemhilde wept or not? She lived on in her arrogance, never thinking that *her* day for grieving was coming on too, slowly but surely.

And now began the dreary round of Kriemhilde's widowhood. She spent a portion of each day alone at her Siegfried's grave. The rest of the time she stayed with her mother, Queen Ute, and her women, but scarcely seemed to heed the anxious kindness with which they waited on her, or to hear the wise and loving words with which they strove to comfort her. No one could win from her a smile, hardly a word, save only her brother Giselher. Four years went by, and she had not spoken once to Gunther; nor had she once met Hagen, her bitterest foe.

Then one day Hagen spoke to the King:

"If you could make friends again with your sister, we might bring over here the treasure of the Nibelungs. It would pay you to do a little coaxing."

"We might try," Gunther agreed; "Gernot and Giselher shall speak for me."

Gernot was the first to try.

"Sister," he said to Kriemhilde the next time he visited her, "you mourn too long for Siegfried's death. The King would show you that he did not kill him if you would but grant him a hearing."

"Nobody ever said he did," she replied. "It was Hagen. For did I not myself make known to him in what spot Siegfried could be wounded? Therefore I can never cease to mourn, nor will I ever meet in kindness those who did or knew of so foul a thing."

Then Giselher began to plead, and him she had not the heart to refuse.

"Very well," she said; "I will speak to the King, since you insist. But you do me a cruel wrong. Gunther has undone me, his own sister, who never did him any harm. My lips may speak forgiveness, but my heart knows nothing of it."

"That will come in time," all her friends encouraged her.

The moment Gunther heard Giselher's report, he went to her with his best friends. Hagen did not dare to present himself.

They met. They spoke. Kriemhilde even was persuaded to suffer the King to kiss her, and many tears were shed. She forgave all, except only the one man.

Not long afterwards they got her consent to bring over the great treasure from the land of the Nibelungs. It was Sieg-

fried's wedding gift to her, and so her own
dower now, to do with as she would.

Giselher and Gernot went for the hoard,
with eight thousand men and many ships.
They took Kriemhilde's order to the
keeper, Alberich the Dwarf, to deliver it
up, and he dared not refuse, for it was
her right.

It took twelve large hay-waggons four
days and nights to cart the treasure from
the mountain cave to the ships, making three trips a day. There was nothing
but gold and precious stones, and in the
middle of the heap was hidden the golden
wishing-rod, which would have made anyone who knew the use of it master over
the whole wide earth and all that it holds,
and every man on it. Many Nibelungs
went as escort to the treasure, for land
and castles and men are all subject to
whoever owns it.

When the hoard was brought to Burgundy and unshipped, it was delivered
over to Kriemhilde, who had it carted to
the palace, where it filled many chambers
and turrets, of which she took the keys.

And yet, had the great treasure been greater a thousandfold, and Siegfried could have been called back to life, and the choice given her, she would never so much as have looked at it, and would have gone to him in her smock. Never hero, of a truth, had so faithful wife.

As it was, she did not herself greatly care for the gold, but she had good use for it. She began to give. She gave to rich and poor, to strangers too: to the poor from kindness, and for the good of her Siegfried's soul; to the rich because she wanted friends devoted to herself, and ready to work her will in due time; that was why brave but needy knights from foreign lands, whom her bounty drew to Worms, and kept there, were especially favoured. She was quietly making a following for herself.

No one interfered with her or seemed to notice her actions. Hagen alone was ever watching her suspiciously. He understood her better than any of the others. He knew that only one thing could have kept her in Burgundy, alone, almost a prisoner, among kinsmen the very sight of whom must be hateful to her, away from her own child and the land where she would have reigned, a queen, among her husband's friends,—and that thing was the hope and purpose of revenge. Therefore, he distrusted everything she did or said, no matter how quiet she kept. And now he tried to arouse Gunther's suspicions also.

"If you let her go on like this a while longer," he said to the King, "she will have so many men in her pay that we shall be in her power."

"Let her alone," Gunther replied, wearily; "the treasure is her own. What right have I to meddle with it or what she does with it? I had enough to do to get her to make friends with me; now I am not going to pry and spy on her and what she does with her own."

"No prudent man will leave such wealth in a woman's hands," Hagen insisted. "If you do not check her lavishness, we Burgundians will yet suffer from it."

"I have sworn an oath," Gunther declared, "never again to do her any harm, or grieve her in any way, and I will keep it. After all, she is my sister."

" *You* need do nothing," said Hagen ; "leave it all to me."

He knew Gunther's moral cowardice, and was not afraid of displeasing him by anything he did by himself. So he watched his chance and stole the keys ; then, once when all the three brothers were absent on an expedition, he had the whole treasure carried away and sunk into a deep hole at the bottom of the Rhine. Giselher had once said in a moment of vexation : " I wish the hoard were at the bottom of the Rhine. Then it would belong to nobody and work no more mischief in the world." And now it was done ; and Hagen bound those who helped him in the work by a strong oath, so long as any of them lived never to tell of the place.

The brothers were very angry when they came back ; Gernot and Giselher really and truly, and Gunther had to pretend he was. Everybody at the court declared it was an outrage, and Hagen thought it best to keep away for a while, the feeling was so strong against him.

Kriemhilde bore the wrong and the loss in silence. She knew complaints would be but a waste of breath. She lived with her mother, even more quietly than before ; and when thirteen years had gone by after Siegfried's death, Queen Ute persuaded her to retire with her to a rich abbey which she had founded and endowed, and where both now thought to end their days in peace and godliness. Only Kriemhilde refused to be separated from him who was her beloved husband dead as he had been alive. So she had his remains removed, with great honour and solemn ceremonies, to Queen Ute's abbey, whither she would have followed immediately herself, but that strange tidings came from far Eastern lands.

XVI

KING ETZEL'S WOOING

IT was about that time that Etzel, the powerful King of the Huns, lost Queen Helke, his well-beloved wife. He mourned her as was seemly; then his friends entreated him to wed again, and advised him to woo the proud widow, Kriemhilde of Burgundy.

"How could that be? objected the King; "I am a heathen, and she is a Christian! She will never hear of it. Only a miracle can bring her here."

"Who knows?" they replied. "Your fame is very great; she may be tempted by that, and by the wealth which is known to be yours. You should try your luck with her, for in sooth she is a noble lady, and should wed with the noblest of all kings."

"Is there anyone among you all," asked Etzel, "who knows the Rhine, the country and the people?"

Then Rudiger, the brave Margrave of Bechlaren, stepped forward and stood before the King:

"I have known from boyhood the three noble kings, Gunther and Gernot, and Giselher, the youngest. Their name is held in high honour and so was that of their father and all their ancestors.

"Friend," King Etzel asked again, "now tell me truly, is she worthy of wearing my crown? Is her beauty really as great as it is said to be?"

"In beauty," Rudiger replied, "she is fully the equal of my late lady, Queen Helke. In the whole wide world no queen can call herself fairer. The man who wins her may well be accounted fortunate."

"Then, Rudiger," cried the King, "woo and win her for me if thou lovest me! Bring her here, and I will reward you richly from my own treasure. And now

you shall take of horses, and splendid garments, and coined gold as much as will
keep you and your comrades in plenty
and merry living on the long journey to
the Rhine."

"Not so," Rudiger replied ; "it would
ill befit me to take aught from your royal
store.   I shall gladly go as your messenger,
but at my own cost.   I am well able to
bear it, and all I own I have from you."

"And when do you think to start?"
asked the King.

Rudiger reflected :

"We must provide ourselves with arms
and clothing ; and I intend to take with
me five hundred knights.   The Burgundians shall confess that no king ever yet
sent so well equipped an embassy so far
from his own land.   And I must see my
dear wife, Gotelinde, and order my house-
hold.   In twenty-four days we shall be
ready to start."

And so it came to pass that just as
Kriemhilde was making ready to join her
mother in the abbey, Rudiger stood before
her brother Gunther and asked for her

hand in the name of his famous master, Etzel, King of the Huns.

He had been well pleased with his reception so far, had met several old friends, of the times when they were all young together, and found right willing ears when he delivered his message. Gunther at once replied :

" If my word has any weight with her, she shall not say your master nay. I will let you know in three days from now."

When Rudiger and his companions had been taken to comfortable quarters and provided for with hospitable care, the princes held a secret council with their most trusted friends. All, to a man, thought it would be a good thing that Kriemhilde should wed King Etzel. Hagen alone thought differently.

" If you are wise," he said to Gunther, "you will take care what you do, and even if she should want to go, you will not let her."

" Why should I not ? " the King asked wonderingly. " Whatever may betide the Queen that is for her good, I shall be only too glad : she is my own sister, and it is for us to look after and care for her."

" You speak but foolishly," Hagen still persisted ; " if you knew Etzel and his power as I do, you would not let her make a friend of him, lest you be the first to rue it."

" I cannot see that," replied the King ; "it lies with me never to go near him, and then he cannot injure me, were he ten times her husband."

But Hagen still repeated, " It is unwise."   Gernot and Giselher were very wroth with him for his ill-natured stubbornness, and rebuked him with bitter words.

" Truly," they said to him, " you have done her such grievous wrong, it is but what you deserve, if she hates you.   And if you had a spark of conscience, you would not grudge her a little late happiness."

Hagen saw that he was entirely alone of his opinion.   But he had the last word :

" I do not deny it.   But I will say to the last that if the noble Kriemhilde wears Helke's crown, she will do us hurt and harm wherever she can. And it behoves you, her brothers, to have a care."

After this, he spoke no more, but sat by, sullen and gloomy; and it was resolved that Kriemhilde should be told of King Etzel's offer and advised to accept it.

Yet, and though all were against Hagen, things very nearly shaped themselves to please him. For Kriemhilde would not hear of wooing or wedding, and at first was inclined to look on her brothers' urging as a mockery. At last she consented to receive Rudiger and not to insult so great a king as Etzel by sending back his messenger unheard.

"Send him to me to-morrow morning," she said, "and I will give him my answer myself. I think highly of Margrave Rudiger. Had it been any other messenger, he should never have had speech of me."

And so next morning she received him and the eleven knights who came with him with great friendliness and courtesy. But she wore her everyday dress, without

9

an ornament, although her women were arrayed in their best, to do the envoy honour. She heard him out patiently, but her answer was ready:

"Margrave Rudiger, if any man living could measure the sorrow which I bear ever within my heart, he would not advise me to wed another man. I lost the best husband woman ever had."

"And what greater comforter can we have in sorrow," the wily envoy retorted, "than friendship and sweet love? And if you deign to accept my noble master's love, know that twelve wealthy crowns will be yours, and for your dower he will give you the lands of thirty princes whom his mighty hand has conquered. And you shall rule over many a worthy knight and many a fair maiden of princely race, who were Queen Helke's own attendants, and all King Etzel's subjects shall be yours, and power imperial, unlimited,—this he bade me tell you."

Kriemhilde grew thoughtful as she listened, then spoke with noble dignity:

"Enough. Press me no more to-day.

Return to-morrow morning, and I will give you my final answer."

She sent for her mother and for her favourite brother, Giselher. She listened to their reasons, then dismissed them without a decisive word, and spent the night alone, in doubt and tearful prayer. Early in the morning, before mass, her brothers visited her, all three, and took her by the hand and lovingly entreated her. Then the Huns were once more introduced. They entered, grave and somewhat stern, for they had come to take their leave unless she changed her mind.

Rudiger, with courtly words, besought the Queen to declare what answer he should take to King Etzel and his people. The answer came, low but clear :

" I never again can love or wed."

From this no words or entreaties could move her. Then Rudiger craved a secret audience of the Queen. They stood apart where none could hear the low-breathed words :

" Cease from weeping. Had you no one in the land of the Huns but myself alone, my vassals and my friends, we should make anyone pay dear who ever had offended you."

She looked up at that, and there was life in her eye.

" Will you swear to me, Rudiger," she said, "that whoever may do me a wrong you will be the first to avenge me ?"

" That will I," he answered readily, and swore the oath and gave his hand on it. She, meanwhile, was thinking in her heart. " If I can win so many devoted friends, I do not care what people may think of my wedding again, for then I can hope at last to avenge my Siegfried's death.   If Etzel has so many liegemen, and I am given power over them, then I can do anything I please.   And he has treasure enough. I can give without stint."   She made a last objection :

" Had I not been informed that he is a heathen, I might possibly think of accepting King Etzel's offer."

" He is not quite a heathen," Rudiger quickly replied ; " he has been baptised— you may believe my word—but he relapsed into paganism. He has as many Christian as heathen subjects, and if he had a Christian wife, who knows but she might incline his heart again to God."

They returned to where her brothers stood and all three urged her again and again, till she sorrowfully gave her consent and held out her hand to Rudiger.

The Margrave was so delighted, he would have liked to carry her away that very day, and would scarcely allow her time for her preparations and farewells. As she was herself anxious to go, now she had made up her mind, it took her less than a week to get herself and her attendants ready. The faithful Margrave Eckewart declared that he would follow her with his five hundred men, so she should not come to the land of the Huns without a royal retinue. He had sworn to her allegiance until death, he said, and only death should part them. A hundred fair maidens of noble birth were chosen to attend her, and the loading of the pack-horses had already begun, when Hagen, with unmannerly insolence, forbade Kriemhilde's people to take away her treasure. It was a portion of the Nibelung hoard which she had kept in her own apartments, and therefore he had been unable to lay his hands on it. Though but a small remnant of the whole, there was still enough to load sixty mules.

"Kriemhilde," he said, "will never forgive me, and I were a fool to leave such wealth in my mortal foe's hands. I know well enough what she would do with it; she would use it all to hire men against me. I will take care of it—you may tell her so from me."

The Queen was angered beyond words, and her brothers were indignant. They would have interfered, but Rudiger would not let them.

"Most royal lady," he said to Kriemhilde, "would you shed tears for the bit of gold? Let King Etzel but lay eyes on you, and he will pour such wealth into your lap that you could never spend it. Were all the treasure still yours that ever was brought from Nibelung, neither your hand nor mine should touch it. Of mine own store I brought so much from home, that we have more than enough for twice the journey."

The parting was not without many tears. Mother and daughter well knew that they were seeing the last of each other ; but her sorest grief was parting from her favourite brother, Giselher. Nor did she refuse a sisterly kiss to Gunther and Gernot, and when at last the well-mounted troop wended its way eastward toward the River Danube, there remained behind many a heavy heart and many a tearful eye. But Gernot and Giselher insisted on escorting her part of the way with one thousand of their bravest knights. Nor did they take leave of her until they stood on the very bank of the Danube, which parts the German lands from those of the Huns. She clung pitifully to her brother Giselher, as he whispered to her : " Sister mine, should you ever have need of me, or should any danger threaten you, send me word, and I will ride forthwith to help you, straight to King Etzel's land."

Then the Burgundians rode away, back to the Rhine.

XVII

IN HUNLAND

FOR thirteen years Kriemhilde had been Queen of the Huns. Never had King Etzel loved Queen Helke as he now loved his wife from Burgundy. Her power over him was unlimited. And when a son was born to them, she found no difficulty in getting the delighted father's consent to have the child baptised and brought up a Christian. She was not less beloved by the country at large ; the Huns all declared they never had had so kind and gracious a queen. For she was gracious by nature, and had made it her special object to win her new people's love. She appeared to be happy and contented, and no one suspected that her whole heart lived in the past with the dead, that life in the strange land was hateful to her, that her only thought and hope, morning, noon, and night, was that of revenge. She was homesick and longed to see her brothers again, Gernot, and especially Giselher, and her old true friends, but she had not forgiven Gunther even though she had given him the kiss of peace, and as for Hagen, she could scarcely wait until she should have him in her power. She was sick with her long-deferred hope and craving, but waited patiently and made no move, until she felt herself so firmly anchored in the love of her husband and people that she could carry through anything she set her mind to. Thirteen years she waited ; then she felt that her time had come. And so one evening, when King Etzel had been par-ticularly good-natured and affectionate, Kriemhilde spoke at last of what had never been out of her mind :

" My loving lord, if I have found favour in your eyes, I would this day ask you for a token. It grieves me that none of my people have visited me in this long time.

Your people here must think I have no friends."

King Etzel answered as she knew he would :

" Sweet wife, if it is not too long a journey for them, I would willingly ask them all here, as many as you would like to see. You will not be more glad to see them than I shall. I have sorrowed more than once that they should keep aloof from us."

Two messengers, with a sufficient escort, were quickly equipped. The King himself gave them their instructions, to which the Queen privately added some of her own. They were never to betray to anyone at her old home that she had ever been seen sad or thoughtful ; they were to let her mother, Queen Ute, know how highly she was honoured among the Huns ; her brother Giselher they were to tell that her eyes ached for a sight of him ; and they were especially to see that Hagen did not stay behind, because, she explained, he alone among the Burgundians knew all the roads to Hunland and was familiar with the country. Gifts and greetings there were for all, even for Brunhilde.

Great was the wonder and turmoil in Burgundy as King Etzel's envoys rode through the land. The rumour of their coming reached Worms much before them and the royal family was anxious to learn what they brought. The invitation was a great surprise to all. The brothers were delighted to hear from their sister; but the question was a weighty one, and King Gunther asked his friends' opinion singly, one by one. Each advised him and his brothers to go, until Hagen's turn came to speak, which he did, angrily and roughly:

"Have you all taken leave of your senses? Have you forgotten what we once did to her? It behoves us to beware of Kriemhilde as long as we live. I slew her husband with this right hand of mine—how then can we go of our own free will to King Etzel's land and put ourselves in her power?"

"Speak for yourself," retorted the King;

"my sister is at peace with us ; in the loving kiss she gave us at parting all malice was forgotten. How you, Hagen, stand with her, you know best."

" Do not deceive yourselves," Hagen warned again, " whatever these Huns may say. If you trust yourselves to Kriemhilde, you will rue it. She knows how to nurse a grudge, King Etzel's noble wife !"

" You may have good cause to fear for your own life among the Huns," Gernot tauntingly put in his word ; "but that is no reason why we should shun our sister."

" And since you feel so guilty, friend Hagen," Giselher chimed in, " you had better stay at home. Only those who feel safe need go to Hunland."

" You know that fear will never keep me at home," growled Hagen, angrily. " If you will not be advised, I will show you whether I am afraid."

Others now began to speak in the same sense as Hagen ; some of the best men roundly refused to go ; Hagen's nephew, Ortewein of Metz, was of the number.

But all this only made Gunther more determined, until Hagen yielded so far as to say :

"Let not my words trouble you. Go if you must. But let me give you this one advice, out of my duty to you : go well prepared."

"That we will !" cried Gunther cheerily, and forthwith sent out a call for three thousand men, all picked and proven warriors.

Hagen and his brother Dankwart brought a thousand of their own men; Folker, the noble minstrel-knight, also came not unattended. But Marshal Ortewein, Hagen's nephew, and several others, absolutely refused to go. They mistrusted Kriemhilde; and as it was necessary that some should stay to take care of the country and to look after Gunther's Queen and children, they were allowed to have their way.

All this time, Etzel's messengers were detained, under one pretence or another, much against their will. But Hagen would not give them more than seven days' start, that Kriemhilde might not have time for much dangerous preparation. At last they were allowed to pay their respects to the aged Queen-mother, after which they were escorted with due honour to the frontier of Burgundy and some way beyond. Brunhilde would not see them, excusing herself with ill health.

When Kriemhilde was told of the messengers' return, she sent for them at once, and after generously rewarding them for their trouble and good news, she asked the names of those who were coming with her brothers, and was especially curious to know what Hagen had said.

" Not much that was pleasant," was the answer ; " when they decided to undertake the journey, he told them they were going to their death."

Kriemhilde sought the King and spoke to him with joyful face and smiling lip :

" Is my dear lord pleased at my news? The only wish I had is now about to be fulfilled."

" Thy will is my pleasure," the King replied affectionately ; " I would not so rejoice in my heart if they were my own best friends who came to visit us."

He hastened to give orders that everything should be made ready for the guests' honourable reception and greatest comfort. Little he knew that their coming was to be the end of all his joys on earth.

XVIII

THE JOURNEY

JUST as the Burgundians were about to start, something happened which rather damped their spirits. Ute, the aged Queen-mother, who had all the time been anxious that her sons should visit their sister, suddenly begged them to change their minds on the very morning appointed for their departure.

"It were best after all you stayed at home," she said to them. "I had a dream last night that bodes no good. I thought all the birds in Burgundy were killed."

They were rather shaken at that. But Hagen was not going to let them stay, now they were all ready to go, on account of an old woman's dream, after they had made light of his sensible objections. He laughed at them and held them to their word. And sorry enough he was for it afterwards.

The journey went on smoothly and merrily as far as the River Danube. They found it swollen, angry, and overflowing its banks—and no ferry in sight. Hagen started to explore the country and see if he could not find one. As he rode about rather aimlessly, he came on two maidens bathing in a quiet creek. He stole up to where their clothes lay on the bank and hid them, for pure mischief, while they swam quickly away.

They were water-maidens, wise in secret lore. They stopped at a distance from the bank and one of them spoke :

"Hagen, noble knight, if you will return our clothes, we will tell you how you will fare on this your journey to the Huns."

This was just what he wanted most to know, so he promised.

"You may ride on nothing daunted," the same water-maiden then said ; "never did heroes ride to greater honours than await you in King Etzel's land, of that rest assured."

Nothing could have pleased him better, so he at once brought back the clothes. Then the other water-maiden spoke:

"Hear my warning, Hagen. My sister spoke only half the truth. Turn back while there is yet time, for death awaits you all in Etzel's land."

"These are but idle threats," Hagen retorted. "What can happen to us in a friendly country, whither we go as invited guests?"

"And yet it is as I say," replied the water-maiden; "not one of you will see his home again, except only the King's chaplain, we know for certain. He will return safe and sound to King Gunther's land; he, and no one else."

With this the maidens left him, sore perplexed. He rode on and came to a ferry, but the ferryman refused to take the men across, although Hagen promised him a generous reward, and offered him a rich golden shoulder-clasp as a free gift. The man said he would not take strangers, who might turn out to be foes and invade his liege lord's lands, saying which he seized his heavy oar, long and broad, and hit Hagen a blow which brought him to his knees. The next moment the ferryman's head flew into the river. Then Hagen fastened a long strap to the boat and towed it to where his friends were encamped, waiting for him. He himself took them across in small parties, the horses swimming alongside. Not one was lost, either man or horse.

With the last party the King's chaplain was preparing to cross; he stood ready, clasping the Sacrament. The moment Hagen's eye fell on the priest, he attacked him furiously, like one suddenly gone mad: "Hold on, Hagen, stop!" a hundred voices shouted at him, but he stayed not his hand until he had forced the priest overboard into the river.

"What makes you want to kill the chaplain?" cried Gernot angrily. "Were it anybody but yourself, he should rue it. What has the man done to you that you should treat him so?"

Hagen answered never a word, but, kept furiously hammering at the priest with an oar, until the poor man, swimming with all his might, succeeded in reaching the bank, which he climbed, then sank down exhausted. As he rose to his feet, shaking the water from his robe, Hagen saw that the water-maiden had spoken the truth, and muttered, "We are lost!"

When all the men and all the luggage had been carried safely to the other side, he began, still silently, to hack the boat in pieces and to throw the pieces into the river.

"Why, brother, what are you doing?" cried Dankwart; "were it not better to conceal the boat, so we can use it again on the homeward journey?"

"There will be no homeward journey," Hagen replied, gloomily; "and if there is any coward among us, who would fain save his skin, he shall lose his life at my hands right here, by this river."

The chaplain who had been looking on from the opposite bank, now spoke in loud and threatening tones, before he turned to start on his way home.

"You caitiff! you dastardly murderer!" he shouted across the water. "What had I done to you that you should want to drown me, a poor harmless priest? Go! go your way to the Huns! I will hie me back to the Rhine—which may you never see again! that is my hearty prayer."

So the Burgundians started on their further journey laden with the good man's curse.

They had fared well so far, and even now nothing of note happened to them, except a skirmish with the lord of the country through which they rode. He heard of the ferryman's death and, thinking that enemies had come to take his land from him, he rode after them in pursuit with some troops, but was slain in the fight which followed, and his men dispersed. No one molested the Burgundians after that and they arrived safe and sound at the boundary of Rudiger's margraviate of Bechlaren. Here they found, on guard, Siegfried's old and trusted friend,

Margrave Eckewart, who had followed Kriemhilde into the land of the Huns. From him they had their first warning.

"Alas, but I am sorely grieved to see you here," he said, after the first greetings; "you best know, Hagen, what you have done, and what welcome you may look for here in the land of the Huns. Keep good watch—that is the best advice I can give you now that you are here. But come; yourselves and your horses must be spent with the long journey and you cannot have many provisions left. Come then; I will take you to a host, the most hospitable you have met in any country. His heart bears kindness as the lovely month of May bears grass and flowers. I will take you to my friend Rudiger."

The good Margrave had not forgotten the friendly reception which he had met with at the Court of Burgundy when he came thither to woo Kriemhilde for his royal master. And now he could not do enough for his guests, on whom he prevailed to remain several days at his castle, until all trace of fatigue should be gone, so they should present themselves before King Etzel well rested and in perfect trim. Their followers were requested to make themselves at home on a vast field near by, where hundreds of tents were erected for their comfort, and all their needs were amply provided for. Rudiger himself, his wife, and his young daughter devoted all their time to the royal brothers and their immediate friends, with whom they exchanged kindnesses and costly gifts, so that a very close friendship had grown up between host and guests—and indeed, Giselher and Rudiger's lovely daughter had become engaged lovers, when he at last announced that he had sent off messengers to inform King Etzel of their arrival and that it might be considered rude if they tarried any longer.

XIX

THE ARRIVAL

BEFORE they reached the royal residence, the Burgundians had one more serious warning. Dietrich, King of Bern, one of the most famous heroes of the age, was at this time paying a visit to the King of the Huns, who requested him, in order to do them the greater honour, to go himself to meet them, with a chosen body of troops. He consented the more willingly that he wished to caution them, and this was the best chance.

The Burgundians, seeing him approach and being told who he was, dismounted to receive him, and so did he.

"Welcome!" he cried, shaking each by the hand as he named him: "welcome, royal Gunther, likewise Gernot, Giselher,

and Hagen, and you, my lords Folker
and Dankwart! But are you not aware
that Kriemhilde has never, to this day,
ceased to weep and mourn for the hero of
the Nibelungs? Let me bid you beware!"

"Let her," replied Hagen, carelessly;
"he has been dead these many years, and
will stay so. She had better think more
of the King of the Huns."

"What should I beware of?" Gunther
joined in. "Etzel sent for us; we have
come trusting to his royal word. And my
sister also sent many loving messages of
her own."

"What more can I say?" replied Dietrich. "All I know is that every morning
I hear her cry and moan, as though her
heart would break, and call to high
Heaven for vengeance on Siegfried's
slayers."

"What is done cannot be undone,"
spoke Folker, the minstrel-knight. "As
things are, nothing is left us but to ride
on to court and see for ourselves."

And now they all rode on together; the

Burgundians in closely serried ranks, with proud and martial bearing, after their country's fashion. The roads were crowded as they passed. The Huns were especially anxious for a look at Hagen, whom they knew to have slain the mightiest of all famous heroes ; the curiosity to see him was great as well at court as through the country. And as they gazed their fill on him, they beheld a middle-aged warrior, powerfully built, broad of chest and shoulders, with dark hair mixed with grey, tall and erect of figure, grim and forbidding of face.

When they arrived, the knights were taken at once to rich and handsome quarters, but not roomy enough to hold their followers also, who were comfortably housed elsewhere. That they were thus separated was due to Kriemhilde's forethought.

The moment she was informed of their coming, she went to visit them with a few attendants. She greeted her brothers, but kissed only Giselher, and never gave a look to Hagen. Seeing which, he made his helmet faster on his head and spoke out loud and roughly :

" After such a reception, our friends may well be in doubt. Greetings, I see, are unlike for prince and subject. We might have spared ourselves the journey."

" Let those welcome you," the Queen retorted sternly, " to whom you are a pleasant sight. As for me—what precious gifts have you brought me from the Rhine, that *I* should give you such a warm welcome ? "

" What foolish talk is this ? " rudely broke in Hagen. " Gifts ! why should we bring you any ? Had I but thought of it, I am not so poor but that I might have presented you with some gewgaw or other."

" One thing only I would ask you," Kriemhilde said tauntingly : " what did you do with the Nibelung treasure ? that was my own, as you know very well. It was your plain duty to bring it to me here."

" Sooth to say, my lady Kriemhilde, it is many and many a day since I am rid of

the nuisance.   My lords, your brothers,
had it sunk in the Rhine, and there it shall
lie until Doomsday."

"Think not at least that I am longing
for the gold; I have more of that than I
could ever spend.   But I am the victim of
a murder and a felony, and for that my
heart craves satisfaction."

Then, turning to all the knights, the
Queen commanded:

"The King's guests may not carry arms
in the King's mansion.   Give yours to me,
ye warriors; I will take care of them."

"That shall never be!" Hagen cried
quickly; "you do us too much honour,
royal lady,—we could not suffer your fair
hands to carry our heavy shields, and other
weapons.   It is not your place: you are
the Queen.   Besides, my father taught me
to take care of my arms myself."

The Queen frowned and bit her lip.

"They have been warned!" she muttered.   "Did I but know who dared to do
it, that man should lose his life."

"*I* did!" Dietrich declared defiantly;
"I warned the noble princes and Hagen,

too, their liegeman.   Do your worst, you fiendish woman ; you dare not touch me."

And he gave her such a look that she flushed with shame and anger, and went without another word, only casting a venomous glance at her foe.

So greatly had years of brooding over one great wrong, and of unholy craving for revenge changed Siegfried's gentle wife !

XX

ON GUARD

THERE was an ominous silence after Kriemhilde had gone. Then Hagen and Dietrich joined hands, and the latter spoke :

"It grieves me much, in truth, that you and your friends should have taken this journey, now the Queen has spoken such words."

"Forewarned, forearmed," was all that Hagen said. And they parted for the time.

The palace in which the Burgundians were housed stood directly opposite the royal palace ; there Kriemhilde stood at a window and could not take her eyes off the gate over the way, before which sat the two friends, Folker and Hagen, mounting guard. Hagen knew she was looking,

and, the deeper to spite her, had laid Siegfried's own good sword, Balmung, across
his knees. She burst into tears at the
sight, and told her great grievance to
those of Etzel's warriors who were in the
same room with her.

"I would be beholden to my dying
day," she concluded, amidst tears and sobs,
"to any man who would avenge me on
that man ; I must have his life."

King Etzel, in the meantime, who had
not the remotest idea of his wife's feelings and evil schemings, was wondering
why his guests were so long in presenting
themselves before him. Then some of
his nearest friends went over to bring
them to court in state. Dietrich of Bern
took Gunther by the hand, Rudiger took
Giselher, others took the rest ; so all walked
in pairs, and, crossing the palace-yard, entered the great audience-hall.

The moment Etzel saw King Gunther,
he sprang from his seat and, meeting him
half way, the two exchanged greetings the
most cordial that ever passed between
crowned heads.

"Welcome!" he cried, "thrice welcome, noble Gunther, and you Gernot, and you, brother Giselher! Welcome also all your knights with you! And you especially be welcome to me and to my wife here, my Queen, ye two worthies from the Rhine, Hagen and Folker the bold. She sent you many a kind message, I know."

"Which were duly given us," replied Hagen, in his courtliest manner. "Had I not come in my liege's following, as in duty bound, I would have taken the journey on purpose to pay my respects to my lord the King."

Once again the King took his dear guests by the hand, and led them to their seats, close by his own. And while the cupbearers filled their wide golden bowls with wine and mead, he once again bade them welcome.

"I must confess," he said, "I often wondered wherein I had failed against you, that, while so many noble guests graced my hearth, you, my brothers, never took the journey to my land. But now I see you here, my joy at having you under my roof and at my board makes me forget the slight sting of former neglect. Let us therefore rejoice and be happy together."

The banquet was splendid beyond words, and would have lasted far into the night, had not the guests pleaded fatigue and asked to be taken to their night-quarters. They found a vast hall lined with most luxurious beds, wide and soft, decked with costliest, daintiest furs, such as ermine and black sable. But, tired as they were, they did not dare to enjoy the rest on these tempting couches. Yet it would have been very unwise for them to meet the morrow's dangers unrested and unrefreshed; so Hagen and Folker volunteered to keep guard at the door of the hall, and bade their comrades sleep.

Half an hour later not a man was up but those two. Hagen sat leaning against the door-post with Balmung lying bare across his knees. But Folker took his fiddle and bow and softly played some of his sweetest tunes, with which he was wont to shorten many a starlit evening at home, by the Rhine. He played to sleep many a careworn soul that night, their last night of kindly rest.

Their fears had not been idle. The night was not half spent when the two faithful watchers heard the clanking of armour and caught a faint glimmer of steel through the darkness. It was a small body of Huns which approached the house and halted at some distance from the gate. Finding it so well guarded, they whispered among themselves and walked softly away, thinking themselves unnoticed. But Folker challenged them, and, receiving no answer, cried after them :

" Fie on the dastards, who would have murdered weary men in their sleep!"

Nothing more happened that night and Hagen woke his comrades as the grey dawn was creeping into the windows of the hall. Presently the church bells began to ring and they were called to early mass. King Etzel attended it with many of his heathen Huns, to do honour to his guests. He was astonished to see them in full armour, with shield and sword and spear, and shining breastplate instead of festive silken robes.

"What is this I see?" he cried. "My friends helmeted and belted? By my troth, if anybody here has offended you, ye shall have satisfaction, in any way ye may yourselves appoint."

To which Hagen replied:

"No one offended us. It is my people's custom to go armed for three full days when they are on a visit."

Kriemhilde shot a furious glance at him from under her lowered lids. If only somebody had had the courage to tell King Etzel how things really were, he would have prevented the disaster. But all were silent, from fear of being rated as tale-bearers, and he alone of all present began the day with a light heart and a mind free from care.

After church the whole forenoon passed away in knightly exercises, a-foot, and a-horseback, in which the Burgundians and the Huns strove to outdo one another. There were many single encontuers, and in the general sham battle which ended the morning's show, the performers, secretly moved as they were by a silent grudge and mutual ill-feeling, came very near making earnest of play. King Etzel, who had been enjoying the exercises from the window at which he sat with Kriemhilde, was astonished and somewhat alarmed. But she looked on unmoved, indeed rather pleased, because she saw that Hagen was fast losing control of himself, and if he happened to be killed, her revenge would have been accomplished without any further action on her part, and she could then peacefully enjoy her brothers' visit, for she did not wish harm to them or any of those who came with them. But it was not to be. The evil seed of so many years was to bring forth its full harvest of evil.

What Etzel feared took place. A Hun of great size and lordly bearing bore down on Folker with such violence that Hagen could not do anything but fight in earnest, in his friend's defence. Others joined in and made a quick end of the Hun. The tumult that followed was deafening; help and arms were called for on all sides, knights were unsaddled, and it took all the King's authority, as he appeared among the rioters, to prevent a general engagement. With his own hand he struck a heavy weapon from the grasp of a cousin of the dead Hun and shouted in a voice of thunder:

" If you had killed that man you should have paid dearly for the deed. That your cousin was slain was an accident; I saw it all. Let not a hair be touched on my guests' heads."

This put an end to the morning's pastime. But the dark mood it had brought forth cast its shadow upon the feast which followed. The King frowned as he saw all his own men appear at table in full armour. He guessed that they were watching their chance to avenge their comrade, and sternly warned them that the peace must be kept.

Meanwhile, and before they all sat down to the feast, Kriemhilde had taken apart Dietrich, the King of Bern, and his uncle, old Hildebrand, and entreated them to help her in her revenge.

"It is only Hagen," she said, "whose life I crave; he who slew my beloved Siegfried. I would not for the world that harm should come to any of the others."

But Dietrich at once and absolutely refused:

"Spare your words, noble Queen. Your request does you little honour: your friends came hither relying on your troth. Siegfried may be avenged, but not by me."

Kriemhilde then, in her despair, turned to King Etzel's younger brother, Bledel, who had always been devoted to her, and by dint of coaxing, tears, and promises, got him to consent to undertake, even though unwillingly, the most unwelcome task. He was to prepare for it at once, and therefore could not be present at the banquet.

But she went in, satisfied at heart, in time to enter the hall with Etzel, as was seemly. For the first time the strain on her mind relaxed so far that she felt some pleasure in entertaining her guests, and sent for her son Ortlieb, whom his uncles from Burgundy had not yet seen.

"See here, my friends," the King joyfully cried, turning to his wife's brothers as the boy approached the table : "this is my child, and your sister's, who will grow up, I trust, to show you his duty and service. If the fruit is like the tree, he will be a man of some worth. The lands of twelve kings will I bestow on him. Though young, his friendship will be worth having. Therefore I would request of your brotherly love, that when you return to your home by the Rhine, you take him with you as your own. Bring him up as beseems a royal youth, after the fashion of your country ; and should anybody in any way wrong you, he will be your ready helper and avenger when he reaches man's estate."

Kriemhilde heard, but said not a word. But Hagen spoke, churlishly and roughly, after his wont.

"Surely," he said, "his noble kinsmen

could wish for no better friend, if he grows up to manhood. Only, as I look at him, the young princeling seems to me but poorly in health. I for one do not expect to be his courtier long."

The King glanced at Hagen : the words cut him to the heart. But he controlled himself and kept his peace. All the King's friends were pained at Hagen's insulting words and it tried them sorely to have to pass them by unchallenged. There was not one in that hall who would not gladly have called him out to mortal combat ; the King would have been the first, had his honour allowed. But a guest is sacred, and he remembered the unwritten law even in this moment of bitterest anger.

XXI

KRIEMHILDE'S REVENGE

THINGS were now balanced so danger-
ously that the first move on either
side must bring them toppling down to a
general catastrophe.   The move came
from the Huns.

While King Etzel and his principal
guests were feasting in the great hall,
sullen and expecting they knew not what,
Gunther's retainers sat around plentifully
laden boards in another hall at some distance from the royal banqueting-hall, and
Dankwart, the marshal, attended to their
needs and kept order among them, as was
his office.

Suddenly before them appeared Bledel,
King Etzel's brother, with a strong fol-

lowing, all armed to the teeth.   Dankwart
received him with smiling welcome, and
at first would not believe him when he
said that he and his men had come to
fight the Burgundians to the death, all on
account of Siegfried's murder long ago.

"Why, my lord Bledel," said Dankwart,
"in what does that concern me and my
friends? I was but a boy at the time,
and had nothing to do with it."

"I know, I know it all," sorrowfully replied the Prince; "it was your brother
Hagen and Gunther the King   Still, you
must all pay for it: such is Kriemhilde's
will. So defend yourselves!"

"Is that how the wind blows?" Dankwart cried angrily; "then I am sorry I
wasted kind words on you!"

And, springing up, he snatched out his
long sharp sword and with one stroke of
it severed Bledel's head from his body.

The hall at once became the scene of a
raging battle. Those who were not quick
enough to get all their arms, picked up
the heavy wooden stools and chairs and
hurled them at the assaulters' heads. At

the uproar which arose, bodies of Huns came trooping in from all quarters and in an hour or so all the Burgundians lay dead or dying on the bloody floor. It seemed a miracle that Dankwart escaped unhurt, and the Huns themselves were so astonished at it that they did not oppose him when he rushed out to carry the dreadful news to the royal banqueting-hall, where he appeared, haggard, panting, blood-besmeared, like a spectre of horror and slaughter.

He stood in the door, sword in hand, unable at first to utter a word, but his looks told his story all too plainly. Hagen knew at once what had happened, as he showed by his questions, and when he heard his brother's brief and breathless answers, he was up in a moment.

" I always knew," he cried, "that Kriemhilde would have her revenge sometime. But this is too much for one life. She shall have some more to pay for—to begin with, the boy!"

Saying which he suddenly drew his sword and with one quick flash cut off young Ortlieb's head, which rolled into Kriemhilde's lap.

This was the signal for a general onslaught, and in a very short time there were quite as many Huns lying killed here in the royal hall as Burgundians in the other one. For the guests were desperate and the door was strongly guarded, so no help could come in from without.

King Etzel and Kriemhilde were stunned and powerless. At last there was a pause, from sheer exhaustion. Then she spoke to Dietrich, and entreated him to help them, to save at least their lives. He had not much hope, still he decided to try, knowing that there was no feud between him and the strangers, and that, indeed, they had been mutually friendly from the moment they had met.

So he sent forth a mighty call, loud and shrill as the blast of a horn, and, standing on a table, began to wave his arms, until Gunther and his friends understood that he would speak to them. They at once commanded silence and attention, and Gunther spoke first:

"Most noble Dietrich, have you received any harm at the hand of any of my friends? I were loth indeed it should be so and am ready to give you any satisfaction."

"No harm have I taken," Dietrich replied, "not so far. Therefore I pray you of your courtesy to let me and my particular friends leave this building under your royal safeguard. If you do, my hand and sword shall ever be as your own."

"Go in peace," said Gunther at once, "and take with you as many as you wish, so they be not of those who are killing my friends, for these must take their chance —we have suffered too much at the hand of the Huns."

Then the King of Bern laid one arm around the trembling Queen and made Etzel take his other arm, and thus led them out of the building, many warriors following them.

The three brothers granted the same privilege to their kind friend and host, Margrave Rudiger; so he also led many warriors from the hall. A piece of chivalrous generosity which was to cost them dear.

After this clearing of the hall not many Huns were left alive in it, and, after another brief fight, their bodies soon lay on the hard floor beside their dead comrades. Then the Burgundians sat down to rest and get their breath, but were up again in a few moments, for they had still a grim piece of work before them ; to carry out the dead, their own and the Huns'. The latter were very many and were laid in high heaps in the street before the palace.

And now the terrible day was done— a long midsummer day. Darkness descended, and with it fear of what the night might bring. Kriemhilde sat gloomy and silent, despair in her heart. It had all come so suddenly and so differently from what she had planned. Hagen alone was to have suffered. He alone was her Siegfried's foe and slayer, and she had never intended that punishment should fall on any other head. But young Bledel had misunderstood her, and thousands had

perished ; and thousands more must per-
ish—there was no stopping it.   And she,
after giving up one child to what she held
a sacred duty, now had lost the other by
the same murderer's hand and brought all
this horrible disaster on the man who had
been so kind a lord and husband to her,
and who, after this day's work, would never
smile again.

Meantime, the Burgundian heroes held
sorrowful counsel together.   They decided
that a quick death would be better than
this long uncertainty.   They sent a messenger to King Etzel, asking him to come
to them and hear something they had to
propose, and the three brothers, as they
were, in their armour, black and grimy
with dust and blood, stepped out before
the palace, to await his coming.

Etzel came.   Not alone—Kriemhilde
came with him.

"What would ye with me ?" the King
spoke sadly and sternly.   "Would ye have
peace ?   That can hardly be now, after ye
have done me and mine such bloody harm.
Not so long as I have breath.   My child

and all my friends whom ye slew must stand forever betwixt you and me."

To which Gunther gave answer:

"We were forced to it. We did not begin. My people were slaughtered at their meal by your warriors. Is that your troth? I came trusting to your pledged word, and holding you my friend."

Then young Giselher addressed those that had come with the King:

"Of you I ask, ye warriors of King Etzel, what do ye charge me with? What had I done to you, coming to your country so joyful and confiding?"

They answered him:

"The city here and the palace are full of thy goodness, and the land. Much would we give, for thy sake, that thou hadst never come among us. Many tears had been spared the women of Worms on the Rhine."

"If you would even now put a stop to the slaughter," Gunther once more spoke to the King, "by my troth, it were well done for all. 'T is most undeserved, God wot! this that is done to us."

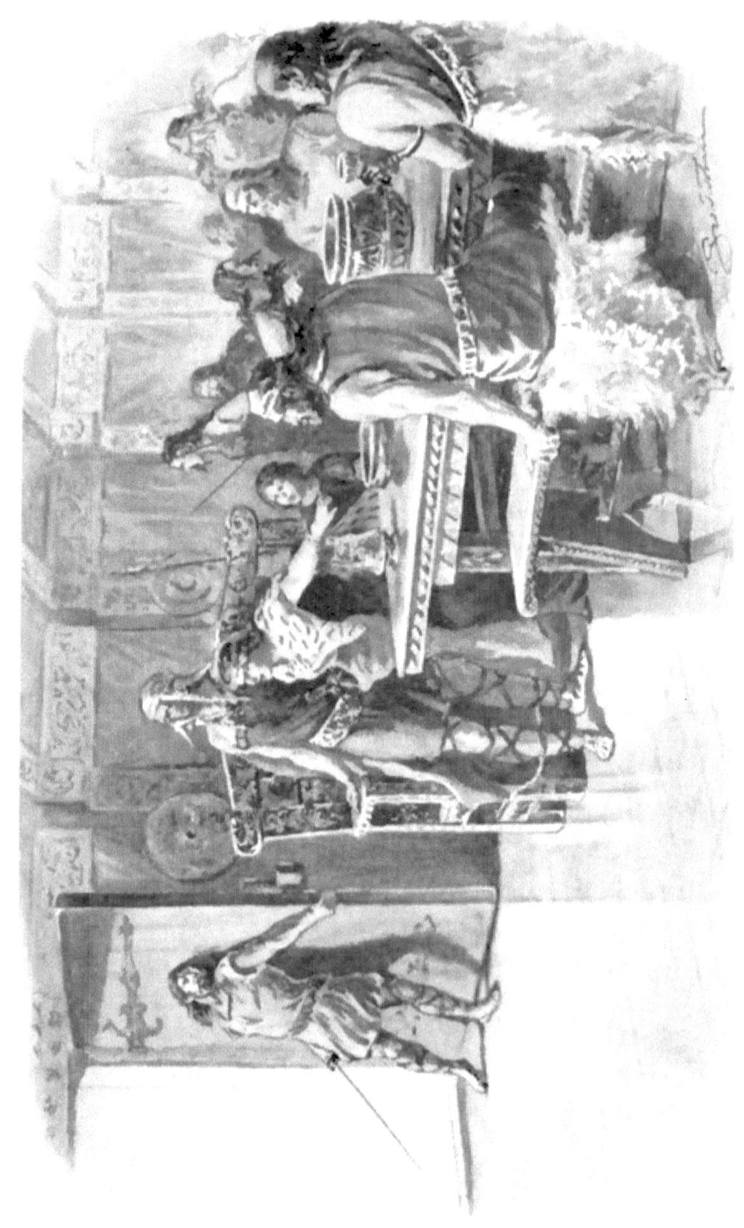

But the host spoke angrily to his former guests :

" Our grievances are most unlike. For the great disaster, the disgrace, and the heartache that ye have brought upon me, not one of you shall escape alive."

Then strong Gernot spoke, with gloomy brow :

" Do us the one favour still : let what must be, be done quickly. Let us out of this hall, to an open place, for our last battle. We are weary unto death, many of us are grievously wounded ; your men are fresh and will finish us promptly. 'Tis better than this long agony."

King Etzel and his men were stirred with pity and about to yield to this request of dying men ; when Kriemhilde, who had hitherto held her peace, cried out, with furious mien :

" Nay, nay, ye warriors ; that were sheer folly, believe me ; I know my mother's noble sons : were they to come alone among you, desperate as they are, ye were lost—the earth never bore braver heroes."

Then sadly spoke young Giselher:

"Fair sister, never would I have believed such treachery of thee, that thou shouldst lure me hither to my death. What have I done to deserve such a fate? Have I not always been a true and loving brother to thee? I came at a word from thee, never doubting thy love. And now I have fallen low indeed, since, sister, I must sue for our lives to thy mercy!"

"I give no mercy where I received none," the Queen pitilessly replied. "Hagen broke my heart at home, and now here he slays my child: for that all must pay who came with him. Still, if ye will deliver him, Hagen, up to me, ye shall live and go hence safe. For ye are my brothers, my mother's children—I mind me of that. Say 'yes,' and I will entreat these warriors to let you go against ransom."

"God in Heaven forbid such felony!" cried Gernot. "Were there a thousand left of us, we should lie down dead at thy friends' feet before we would give up one man to thee."

" We must all die," Giselher joined in ; "then let none say of us hereafter that we could be bribed from usage and law of chivalry. If any would fight us, weakened as we are, they will find us willing ; but I never yet betrayed a friend, and it is too late to begin now."

Then Kriemhilde, blinded by wrath, maddened by her long-deferred revenge, did a monstrous thing : she ordered the building set on fire at the four corners. King Etzel did not gainsay, and many willing hands obeyed the cruel command. As the flames leaped up, all walked away into the night, leaving the wretched victims to their doom.

But the end was not yet. The building was strong, with vaulted roof, the night was still : so the blaze played idly around roof and gable and, though it kept the men within busy all night watching and putting out the firebrands which kept dropping down into the hall and on their helmeted heads, no serious damage was done, and when, soon after daybreak, a body of warriors sent by Kriemhilde approached what they expected to find a smoking heap of ruins, they were amazed to see the walls still standing and hardly injured, and to be met by several hundreds of desperate men. The Huns hastily sent back for more men of the best, even while they began the last fierce battle. It was like fighting men already dead ; yet many a Hun had to lose his life at the hand of the Burgundians at bay, whose only wish was now to send as many as possible to the other world before them.

Rudiger and Dietrich had kept out of the fray until this last hour, for there were strong bonds of friendship and hospitality between them and the guests from the Rhine. While the three royal brothers had been entertained at the Margrave's castle, a marriage had even been arranged between the general favourite, Giselher, and the host's only daughter. Rudiger was to return with them to Worms, where the wedding was to have taken place. And now, in this last hour of extremest peril, he sent a messenger to Dietrich, asking whether he could think of anything to save the lives of the kings even yet, Brief and stern came the reply: "King Etzel will not hear of mercy. And who can gainsay him?"

Then Rudiger wept where he stood.

A gigantic Hun drew the Queen's attention to him.

"See him stand there," he cried, in loud, jeering tone: "he whom you and King Etzel have raised above all other men. Of his many castles, how many were given him by the King? Yet I do not see that he has struck a blow to help us in our sore plight. What cares he, so his house and barns are full! Men say he is the bravest of the brave. We have not seen much of it so far."

The Margrave heard, and regarded the Hun with ominous calmness. Then, stepping up to him and lifting his powerful arm, "Caitiff! take that!" he said,— and struck him one blow on the head with his fist. The man fell prone at his feet— dead.

"That was not well done, noble Rudiger," King Etzel spoke, gloomily; "methinks we had enough dead here as it was. That is a poor kind of help."

"The time was ill chosen to cast in my teeth the benefits I have received from you, and throw a doubt on my honour," retorted the Christian. "He will lie no more."

The Queen looked at Rudiger sadly. Her eyes filled with tears. At last she spoke:

"Have we deserved this of you, the King and I, that you should add to our sorrow? Have you not sworn over and over again to venture for us your honour and your life? And I—I now demand of you the faith which you swore to me with lip and hand when you pressed me to accept King Etzel's wooing, and pledged yourself in my bitter need to serve me until death, to further my vengeance and take all my woe from me."

"And have I not been ever ready to serve you in all things?" Rudiger murmured, sore stung by this reminder. "I will not deny, O Queen," he went on, more firmly, "all that I swore to you. Honour and life I am willing to give for you.   But I did not swear away my soul. 'Twas I who brought the princes to this court!   'Twas me they trusted—my pledged faith!"

Then Etzel also began to entreat, and at last both threw themselves at his feet.

"Oh, woe is me!" cried the tortured man, "that I should live to see this miserable day!   Honour, truth, God's own law—am I to cast them all from me?   O Lord of Heaven, let me die first!   Or send me Thy light, that I may see where duty lies!"

Then suddenly turning to the King—

"Lord Etzel!" he exclaimed, "take back all that thou gavest me : castles, and lands, and gold.   I want nothing.   I will go forth on foot, a beggar, taking only my wife and daughter by the hand, before I end my life by a deed of eternal shame."

But the King would not listen.

"What are lands, and castles, and gold!"

he cried; "it is thy valour, thy manhood, I want, for who else is there to help me in my need? A king will I make thee, a king second only to myself—but help me, now, Rudiger—avenge me!"

"How *can* I hurt them?" the Margrave went on, unheeding the King's words. "They have been my guests, have eaten and drunk at my board, and borne away my gifts. Nay, my daughter I gave to young Giselher—more nobly and virtuously she could never have mated—and shall mine be the hand to slay them?"

But when the Queen once more insisted, entreating his service, not as a due, but as a boon, he could not allow personal affection to stand any longer in the way of his oath and of his duty as vassal to the King of the Huns. He threw both life and soul into the balance.

"I must even keep my oath," he sighed. "Alas, my friends! . . . But one thing is sure: I may not survive this day. Before night my lands and castles shall be yours once more, Lord Etzel, to bestow on whom you will. Therefore, to you I commend my wife and child, and all the homeless ones at Bechlaren."

With heavy step and drooping head he left the King, and went where his five hundred men stood awaiting his orders.

"Arm yourselves," he commanded briefly; "we must fight the brave Burgundians, more 's the pity."

When the three brothers saw Rudiger enter the hall with his following, they greeted him with a shout of joy, for they thought he came as a friend and brought them relief. But the Margrave stood stern and sad for one moment, then cried out to them:

"Brave Nibelungs, defend yourselves! We have been friends—we are so no more!"

An awed silence fell on the Burgundians. They did not believe him.

"Heaven forbid," spoke Gunther at length, "that you should be thus false to friendship and hospitality! You cannot mean it."

"It cannot be helped," replied Rudiger, sorrowfully. "I once swore an oath, and now I am held to it. The Queen leaves me no choice."

"You cannot take our lives, you who have been our kind host and loving friend," said Gunther, still incredulous. "Remember, noble Rudiger, it was you who brought us to Etzel's kingdom."

"And see," said Gernot, "I wear the sword you gave me. It has done me good service this day. And shall I now turn it against the giver?"

"Your wife, the Lady Gotelinde," fell in Hagen, "gave me the shield I brought to Etzel's Court; the Huns have hacked it to pieces, and now I am defenceless. Would that I had one like that one of yours, noble Rudiger!"

"Take it, Hagen," the Margrave said, and held it out to him; "and would to God you might carry it home to Burgundy!"

There was not a dry eye among the doomed warriors; many wept outright. Even Hagen, grim as he was, and hard of heart, was touched at so much gentleness.

"God requite you, noble Margrave," he cried; "there is no other man like you. We had enough heartache to bear without having to fight our friend!"

It was Rudiger's last gift; the hand whose delight it had been to give was never to give any more.

The grief, the suspense, were growing unbearable—an end must be made. Rudiger, who had meanwhile been handed another shield, raised it as a signal to his men, and, loth as they all were, they rushed forward, and the deadly fighting began once more. Rudiger seemed suddenly possessed with the very fury of battle. Headlong he threw himself wherever the fray was thickest. Alas! he killed, but far more was he bent on being killed. The Burgundian chiefs, not one of whom but had received some kindness from his hands, were careful not to cross swords with him, and even of the others many stood aside to let him pass. But he plunged blindly on into the throng, dealing his mighty blows, and each of them was death—till he suddenly found himself face to face with Gernot. By this time the blood of both was up.

"Hold!" cried the Burgundian prince; "wouldst leave me not one man, most noble Rudiger? Nay then, stand and face me! I shall do my best to earn thy gift this day."

Without another word they closed, heroes well matched both. Had it been a knightly contest in the lists, or even a single combat after the rules of chivalry, how would the lookers-on have applauded the splendid lesson in swordsmanship! But this was deadly earnest, and no one heeded the two until, after several wounds given and taken, both made a desperate onslaught, and both fell, mortally stricken, each by the other's hand : Rudiger's gift had found the giver's heart.

Now indeed a hush fell on friend and foe ; but not for long. The Burgundians seemed to gather strength from their despair and made short work of the few remaining followers of the Margrave : in a few moments not one was left alive.

Then only did the leaders—Gunther and

Hagen, and heart-broken Giselher, also Dankwart and Folker, the brave minstrel-knight—gather around the spot where lay the two (now neither friends nor foes), who but three short days ago would have died one for the other. None spoke. Only Giselher said wearily :

"Death hath played sad havoc with us. But cease your weeping and let us go out for a breath of cool air. It will be our turn soon."

Then there was a great stillness in the hall. Some sat down, some leaned against the walls. Etzel and Kriemhilde, who were listening for the end, became impatient and uneasy.

"They must be talking !" the Queen exclaimed at last. "No harm will ever come to our foes from Rudiger's hand. You will see that he will take them all safe and sound home to Burgundy."

But too soon the tidings reached them, and the Queen was shamed, that she had wronged him in her thoughts. Bitterly she wept ; King Etzel's plaint was as a lion's roar ; men's deep moans and women's loud sobbing filled the palace, and all for a time acted as demented with grief.

Dietrich, the noble King of Bern, was the only one who spoke a good word for the Burgundians. He tried to keep back his knights, who began at once to arm themselves and would have rushed to avenge the Margrave's death on the few that were left, without waiting for their liege lord's command.

" Be not so hasty, faithful vassals mine," he implored them. " Whatever has been done by these homeless ones, bear in mind it was not of their seeking : they were forced to it. Let me try to make terms for them, and grudge them not their life and free departure, if so be I can obtain so much."

But he could not hold his men, and though he would not go with them, he allowed them to depart, led by his uncle, brave old Hildebrand, in whose wisdom and kindliness he placed great trust, and who had promised only to ask leave to carry away Rudiger's body. For himself, he sat down in a window, to wait, hoping against hope that he might even yet be of use at the very last moment.

And as he waited, he heard a great rumour in the hall across the way, and he knew there was fighting again. It was some time before Hildebrand stood before him, alone—and wounded.

"Uncle!" Dietrich cried, "what means this blood? Are you hurt? Who did it? You have been fighting with the guests! You should have kept the peace, as I so urgently commanded."

"It was Hagen," the old man replied. "He would have killed me but that I made my escape. I did not think it shame to fly from Siegfried's Nibelung sword, Balmung."

"It served you right," angrily retorted the King of Bern. "You heard me say I would befriend the heroes, and yet you broke the peace which I had promised them. Were it anyone but you, he should pay for it with his life."

"Dietrich," the old man said sadly, "do not be too wroth with me : our friends and I have suffered too much as it is. All we wanted was to carry Rudiger out of the hall, but Gunther's people would not let us."

" Then I must go myself," Dietrich said, rising. " Tell my men to be ready to go with me—and let them bring me my silver armour. I shall hold parley myself with the heroes from Burgundy."

" *Who* is to go with you ?" Hildebrand asked, bitterly : " What is left alive of your men you see before you. The others are all dead. And of the Burgundians only Gunther and Hagen are left."

Dietrich turned pale :

" O my God !" he murmured with quivering lip, " Thou hast indeed forsaken me. But yesterday I was a powerful king ; to-day I am a friendless exile ! . . . Dead ! Bold Helferich,—my well-beloved Wolfhart,—and all my trusty ones—dead ! All in one day ! Shall I ever cease from mourning ? Oh, woe is me that men do not die of grief !"

He went to look for his armour himself ; old Hildebrand buckled it on for him.

Then the strong man broke into such loud lamenting, that the walls were shaken with the voice of his sorrow. But he quickly recovered control over himself, and, firmly grasping his shield, he beckoned to Hildebrand and both walked over to the fateful hall.

Gunther and Hagen were leaning idly against the outer wall.

" There comes Dietrich," said Hagen ; " of a surety he is bent on settling accounts for the great harm we have done him. Well, it is his right ; and if he thinks himself a match for me, king and hero as he is, I am his man."

But Dietrich, as he stopped before the two, set down his shield, and addressed them in mild and sorrowful tones :

" Gunther, what set you so against me, an exile in a strange land like yourself ? What had I ever done to you, that you should take from me all that made life dear ? Was it not enough that ye slew our noble Rudiger, but ye must grudge me my friends ? Truly, never would I have done the like by you !"

" We are not so much to blame as you think," Hagen replied ; " your men came here armed to the teeth, making a great show of their numbers. You have heard only one side."

" What else can I believe ? " said the King of Bern. " My men asked you to let them bear Rudiger away, and ye answered them with gibes and insults."

" It was I would not let them have Rudiger," fell in Gunther ; " I meant to defy Etzel, not your men or you ; but they began to abuse and mock us."

Spoke Dietrich sadly :

" It had to be. But now, Gunther, noble King, I entreat thee by thy chivalry —make me amends for the heartache thou hast caused me, and it shall go unavenged : Surrender thyself and Hagen as my prisoners, and I will engage that no one among the Huns does you any harm. Ye shall find a good friend and true in me."

" Heaven forefend," replied Hagen. " that two men should surrender who stand before thee scatheless and armed : that were cowardice and dishonour."

"I give you my word—and here my hand on it !—that myself will ride with you to your home ; I will escort you thither in honour and in safety, unless I die myself. For your sakes I will forget my own great loss and grief."

" Heaven knows, my lord Hagen," warned old Hildebrand, " the hour may strike only too soon, when you would be glad to take King Dietrich's offer, and it may then be too late."

" I will take my chance of that," cried Hagen ; " not broken as yet is the sword of the Nibelungs. I think it shame that we two should have been asked to sur- render to only two men."

Even as he spoke Hagen sprang against Dietrich with such a mighty leap that the hero was barely in time to raise his shield to catch the Nibelung sword's resounding stroke. In sheer self-defence he struck back and inflicted a gash both deep and broad. But he fought shy of Balmung's magic ; and besides, he thought it would do him little honour to slay a man weak- ened by the long strain on his strength.

So he dropped his shield and sword and, throwing his arms around Hagen, closed with him and wrestled till the Burgundian's last strength gave way and he could bind him for safety.

Then came King Gunther's turn. His splendid courage and skill in arms still held out through a long combat, until he too was wounded, then disarmed and bound like Hagen. It went against the noble Dietrich's heart to treat two such heroes in such unknightly wise, but he knew that, wounded as they were, they would, if free of limb, slay any man they came across.

Dietrich took his two prisoners where Kriemhilde sat. She made no sign, but merely spoke:

"King Gunther, you are very welcome."

To which he replied:

"I would thank you for your greeting, royal sister, were it meant in kindness. But knowing, O Queen, the temper of your mood, I must even take it as a bitter mockery."

Then said the King of Bern :

" Most gracious, royal lady, never yet were such heroes taken prisoners in knightly single combat as these I here entrust unto your care. Let my friendship and services speak for them and gain them favour in your eyes."

Kriemhilde promised with gracious mien. Then, when Dietrich, with tears in his eyes, had taken leave of them, as he thought, for a short time, she did a wicked, shameful deed. For all womanhood was now dead in her.

She had the two locked up separately. Then she went into Hagen's prison and spoke to him shortly and sternly :

" If you will restore to me what you have robbed me of, you may, for Dietrich's sake, go back alive to Burgundy.

Grim Hagen answered as briefly and sternly :

" Lady, you are wasting your words. I have sworn an oath, not to tell where the treasure lies hid. So long as one of my liege lords is living, no one shall have it."

Kriemhilde went out and ordered Gunther to be put to death, and his head cut off. That bloody head she then took up by the hair and carried it in to Hagen.

When the hapless prisoner beheld his beloved lord's head, he drew himself up and spoke with cold contempt:

"All has come about as I foresaw. Thou hast now accomplished thy fell purpose. The noble King of Burgundy is dead. Dead are young Giselher, and Gernot the strong. No one now knows the treasure's hiding-place save God alone and me. And never, thou fiend of a woman, shall it be known to thee."

"Then," she cried, "of all that thou hast taken from me, I shall keep at least my Siegfried's sword, which he wore the last time I ever saw him."

She spoke; and quick as thought she drew Balmung from the scabbard and, lifting it high, struck off Hagen's head. King Etzel saw—but it was done before he could stay her arm.

"Oh woe!" he cried, "that one of the bravest champions who ever fought in battle and carried shield should fall thus by a woman's hand! Much as I hated him, I cannot but sorrow for him."

Old Hildebrand then said :

"It shall not profit her that she succeeded in killing him. Although he slew many of my friends and put me myself in danger of my life, I will avenge him, for he was a brave man."

With this he sprang on Kriemhilde and smote her with his sword. She gave one cry and fell dead among the dead.

Dietrich and Etzel wept aloud, and their friends raised a piteous wail to Heaven.

This is the Lay of the Nibelungs—the story of Siegfried, the hero of the North, and of Kriemhilde's great revenge. As for the Nibelung treasure, it was never heard of from that day to this. There is a spot on the Rhine where popular tradition will have it that the deep hole is, in the bottom of the river, into which the hoard was sunk. But we may be very sure that it will never be explored and that the accursed gold will do no more mischief in the world.

NOTE ON THE " NIBELUNGENLIED "

WHO wrote the Lay of the Nibelungs?
There has been no lack of curiosity, of conjecture, concerning this question, and it is always in a tone of regret that critics and historians admit that it must remain unanswered. As if it mattered! Do we ask after the names of those who wrote the folk-songs and folk-ballads, words and music? Besides, they were never *written*, neither was the epic—they were *written down*, the songs probably unaltered, for music and lyric are spontaneous; the epic was put into shape in the process, which may have beguiled the long leisures of the cloister, the briefer ones of court life—or of camp and march. Possibly all these. For it is very certain that the Lay, as we have it, is the work of more than one pen. This is shown by

the unequal merit of the several parts, some of which drag noticeably as regards interest of incident, spirited narrative, and dramatic vividness of detail ; but it is even more evident from certain contradictions which strike the reader of the unabridged poem, and from the differences between the three extant complete manuscripts, which are not even all of equal length.

Of these manuscripts, docketed *A*, *B*, and *C*, respectively, two are dated from the thirteenth century ; the third is even more recent, and bears the stamp of rehandling by some follower of the artificial school known as " Court-poets "(*Höfische Poesie*). MS. *A* is to be found in the public library at Munich, while *B* reposes in the library of the famous Abbey of St. Gall in Switzerland (not far south of the Lake of Constance - Bodensee). Some critics consider *A* as the oldest and most authentic MS., while others give the preference to *B*. The former have on their side the weighty authority of Lachmann, a follower of the so-called "ballad-theory" in epic poetry, initiated by the great Wolf,—a

theory which denies all individual authorship to the national epics, deriving them
entirely from old folk-ballads, recited by
itinerant minstrels and, in the course
of time, more or less loosely strung together and written down. Although carried by some over-zealous disciples to
unjustifiable lengths, the " ballad-theory "
(*Lieder-Theorie*), is in so far universally accepted, as it accounts for the *materials* out
of which national epics elaborated themselves until the time when they were ripe
for the skilled hands—one or a few—
which were to sift, sort, order them, and
re-cast them into a harmonious literary
whole. If these " hands " happened to
have genius besides, like the problematic
Greek whom we call Homer, and, in a
lesser degree, the unknown poets of
several portions of the Nibelungenlied—
so much the better for posterity.

The heroic and mythic material out of
which the Lay grew is not far to seek.
The cycle of Northern Sagas preserved in
that marvellous Edda which so strangely
came to light in remote Iceland, the last

—and late—stronghold of Northern paganism, in the very thirteenth century of which the two principal Nibelung manuscripts bear the date, tells us all about Sigurd the demigod, with his magic sword, Brynhilde the Valkyrie, fair Gudrun and her brothers, Gunnar and Högni, by the Rhine—and those earlier happenings in the world of the gods and giants, by which we trace the whole wonderful phantasmagoria to the primeval, universal nature-myth of sun and earth, spring and winter. But surely when Christian minstrels, in Christian castles and courts, sang or recited this or that incident from the adventures of the Christian hero, Siegfried of the Netherlands,—at the Christian court of Gunther, King of Burgundy,—his winning of Brunhilde, the fierce maiden of Iceland, for his friend,—his own wooing and wedding of the gentle Kriemhilde, that friend's sister, etc.,—they were all unconscious of the heathen, mythico-heroic substratum, which yet is very perceptible in the finished poem up to the killing of Siegfried by Hagen, *i. e.*, through the first half of it. Nothing here is historic but the setting—the court and chivalry of Burgundy in the fifth century A.D.,—and the name of Gunther. It is probable that this choice of time and place was suggested to the unconscious modernisers of the material by a mere similarity of names: Gunnar—Gunther, the "Gundicarius" of the Latin chroniclers, who was killed in 437, in a hard-fought and bloody battle, by Huns, probably led by Attila, with (it is said) twenty thousand of his own people. This Gundicarius—really Gundahari, later changed into Gunther, was the founder of the first German kingdom on land belonging to the Roman Empire. No wonder if such a personality and such an event became matter for minstrelsy—nor if, in the course of time, both became transformed and absorbed into the older, vaster, and more universally national epic material.

The connexion, however, between Gunther and his vanquisher, Attila, exists already in the original Sigurd-saga. There also Atli (Attila), King of the Huns, weds the hero's widow (Gudrun) and causes the death of her two brothers, Gunnar and Högni (the Hagen of the Lay), by treacherously luring them to his court for a friendly visit, then falling upon them and their retinue with overpowering numbers. The historical, normal nature of the event —war for conquest—being obliterated, it became necessary to supply a motive for the main fact which survived—the killing of Gunnar by Atli ; and the most plausible, nay lawful motive which suggested itself in those ages was revenge. So, with the delicious incongruity characteristic of mediæval story-telling, Atli, King of the Huns, (the Etzel of the Lay) became the brother of the Heaven-born war-maiden Brynhilde, whose dereliction by Siegfried for Gudrun, (though unconscious, owing to a magic potion producing oblivion), he, after many years, avenges— not on Gudrun, a woman and his wife, but on her next of kin, a proceeding entirely in accordance with the Northmen's ancient moral code. Gudrun in her turn, and quite as properly, avenges her brothers, but with hideous refinement of barbarity :

Medea-like, she kills with her own hand
her and Atli's two children, serves their
hearts at supper to the unconscious father,
and, after seeing him partake of the horrible food, murders him in his cups.   This
last is another of those unexpected touches
of history, or at least historic tradition :
for the Goths would have it that Attila
was murdered by a beautiful young German captive, with whom he was so infatu-
ated as to make her his wife, almost at his
wedding feast. They gave the girl's name
as " Ildico "—which of course is no other
than " Hilde "; and herewith we have
the connecting link between the Gudrun
of the older saga, and the " Kriem*hilde* "
of the finished Lay.   In the latter, too,
the motive for the slaughter of the Burgundians at Attila's (Etzel's) court is supplied more plausibly by the murder of
Siegfried, whose widow is his natural
avenger.   So the final tragedy is brought
about by her, not by Etzel, who is only
involved in it ; the greatest horror of it
is thus somewhat mitigated, inasmuch as
we are spared Gudrun's unnatural crimes,

Kriemhilde's and Etzel's child being slain indeed, but by Hagen, in retaliation of the first attack on his friends. Besides, the Lay makes it very clear that Kriemhilde had at first no intention to harm the Burgundians or their chiefs—not even her brother Gunther, whom she had suspected of conniving at Siegfried's death, but had forgiven—and that her vengeance is aimed wholly at Hagen, the villain whose brain planned and whose hand executed the foul deed. That she loses all control of the demon she has conjured up and is herself dragged into the vortex until she is caught in her own murderous engine, and hurried along, half demented, through more and more crimes, more and more innocent blood, even that of her own dearest friends, to the inexorable end—that is the finest moral of the poem, a moral which suggests the text, " Vengeance is mine, I will repay, saith the Lord," and is all the more effective that it emanates spontaneously from the events and characters, instead of these being intentionally shaped to point it.

Next to the Margrave Rudiger, the noblest and most sympathetic figure in the second part of the Lay is the hero-king, Dietrich of Bern; an unmistakably historic one, no other than Theodoric the Great, King of the Ostrogoths (East Goths), surnamed "of Verona" (Bern) because of the decisive pitched battle which he won near that city and which made him the master of Italy. His personality and deeds impressed themselves so deeply on his time and race that he became the centre of an epic cycle of his own. One wonders somewhat to find him at the court of Attila, since he was born in the year of Attila's death (453). Such a slight anachronism, however, would not be considered an obstacle by a mediæval minstrel if the personage otherwise "fitted into" his tale. It is rather more puzzling that he should be represented as occupying a half-dependent position at the side of the King of the Huns, whose claim on his service as vassal he tacitly admits, speaking of himself as a "powerful king" and in the same breath as a "friendless exile."

The historical foundation of this seeming inconsistency must lie in the fact that the Ostrogoths, before Theodoric led them to independence, then to victory and conquests, had been forced to submit to Attila on certain onerous terms, under which they were compelled to fight in his hosts, probably as reluctantly as the contingents of subjected European nations fought in Napoleon's armies. However that may be, in the bloody battle of Châlons, which stemmed the tide of invasion and saved the Christian West, the Ostrogoths were found fighting on the wrong side.

Criticism of the poem is not an object of this notice. Its greatest beauties of incident or character will surely be found self-evident; likewise the beautiful or pathetic touches of detail, such as the first meeting of the two Queens,—that of the radiant young lovers, Siegfried and Kriemhilde,—the death scene of Siegfried in the forest, when his blood dyes the wild-flowers red, as in Kriemhilde's dream,—or Folker, the minstrel-knight, keeping sad guard with Hagen, and softly playing his doomed comrades to sleep with soothing tunes from home, that they may have one last peaceful night's rest before the morrow's combat, the end of which is a foregone conclusion. One thing is certain : there is nothing finer or more pathetic in Homer than the conflict of duties in Rudiger's soul and his despair when loyalty to his King and his oath compel him to do battle without quarter against those who have been his honoured guests and well-beloved friends,—or his last parley with those friends, and his deliberate seeking of expiation in death at their hands.

BEOWULF

THE HERO OF THE ANGLO-SAXONS

PROLOGUE

AMONG the nations of the far North, there was none braver, more hardy, nobler, than the Danes—none whose deeds in war were sung of more proudly at the feasts of earl and thane. Many were the kings whose names came from the inspired lips of Skalds, as their hands struck the stringed harp, in warlike or in mournful chords ; but of these names none were treasured more reverently than those of the Skyldings, the oldest royal house known to Danish tradition. It is a very long time—over a thousand years—since the Danes ruled in England. Yet even then the deeds of the Skyldings were tales of long ago. So long ago that they had become mixed up with much fable ; and especially the beginnings of the famous race were so intertwined with the wonders of heathen Scandinavian antiquity that it has never been possible to decide exactly how much was history and how much myth.

The father of the race, Skyld of the Sheaf, was great in the memory of his people. With his nobles—his ethelings— he had wrested lands and glory from many a neighbouring tribe—aye, and many a distant one, too; the dread of him fell on the bravest warriors; he waxed great under the sun, he flourished in peace, till that every one of the neighbouring peoples over the sea was constrained to obey him and pay tribute; and the world said of him when he died, "That was a good king!"

Yet Skyld was not born to the crown. In fact no one knew anything of his birth and parentage. He was sent, it was said, just when the country had need of a deliverer and leader. He had come one day,—so the story ran,—over the sea, in a beautiful ship, a new-born infant, bedded on sheaves of wheat, when the Danish

people were in sore distress because of
the wickedness of the man who was, at
the time, king over them.

This man's name, Heremod, went down,
unforgotten, but unhonoured, through
many a generation, a by-word for bad
monarchs. He was, in everything, the di-
rect contrary of what a good ruler ought
to be. He used his power, not for his
nobles' benefit or pleasure, but to deal
them wanton harm and even death. For
his ungovernable temper grew on him,
until, in his furious fits, he would strike
and kill, though it were his closest followers, his companions at the board and in
the battle. In his soul there grew a
bloodthirsty passion, and he suffered the
penalty of his evil doings in the estrange-
ment of his friends, the settled dislike of
his people, until at last they would stand
his presence no longer, and he wandered
forth alone, away from all human society,
and was never heard of more. It was
then that Skyld, the mysterious found-
ling, the Heaven-sent, seized on the government, brought order and plenty into

the land, and won love from his people, respect from his foes.

A son was born to King Skyld in his prime, a beautiful child, whom God sent for the people's comfort and solace— Beowulf, sole heir to the throne. From his earliest years he was full of promise, a model of what a young chief should be while still in his father's care— always ready with gracious words and open hand, so that in his riper age will- ing comrades in return were ready to stand by him in war, and men gladly did his bidding. Then, surrounded and assisted by devoted friends who grew up with him, he was enabled to perform deeds which filled the world with praise of him.

As for Skyld, he departed, in the ful- ness of time, ripe in honours and years, to go into the Master's keeping. His faithful comrades then carried him forth to the shore of the sea, as he himself had ordered. The black, heavy earth should have no part in him ; the sea had brought him, the ever-moving, many-hued ; the sea should bear him hence, after his long years of power.

There at anchor rode the ship, glistening fresh, outward bound, fit for a prince. Down they laid their illustrious dead, the dear chief of the land, dispenser of bounties, on the lap of the ship, by the mast. There was great store of precious things; ornaments from remote parts, weapons of rare worth, mail armour finely wrought, and harness glittering in silver and in gold; a multitude of treasures, which were to pass with him far away into the watery realm. Furthermore they set by him the royal banner, gold-broidered, high over his head. As its folds unfurled and glittered in the breeze, it told the skies, and the sun, and the stars of night, that a King went forth into the world, on his last voyage. They set the helm, and gave him over to the ocean, sad at heart, with tear-dimmed eyes, and silent in their mourning. And Who received that burthen— no man under heaven, be it priest or chieftain or wise seer, can ever tell or know.

Thus Skyld of the Sheaf was honoured

in death after the manner of the mighty
dead of oldest times among the strong-
hearted sons of the North.   From the
Unknown he came and into the Unknown
was borne away.

LAY I

GRENDEL

I

HEOROT

THEN Beowulf of the Skyldings sat in
the seat of his father, loved of his
people, for a long time famous among the
nations, and was succeeded in turn by his
son. The royal race of the Skyldings
prospered greatly, and when the crown
came to his grandson Hrothgar, its great-
ness seemed assured for all time. Hrothgar was a youth of goodly parts; brave
and ambitious in war, yet delighting in
the gentle works of peace, a born com-
mander always. So that his brothers and
cousins gladly took him for their leader,

and a young brood of devoted clansmen grew up around him, valiant in battle, merry companions at the board. With these he did some mighty deeds, winning renown and riches, when they were young together, and as together they grew old, he loved to sit with them at the feast, enjoying well-earned rest, rehearsing the toils and joys of the brave old days, and listening to sweet minstrelsy from the lips of God-inspired bards.

Now Hrothgar was very wealthy and his comrades were too many for an ordinary hall, even that of a king's palace. So he bethought him of having men build for him a great banqueting-hall, greater than the children of men had ever heard tell of, that he might spend there happy, careless days, dealing out freely to old and young the goods that God had blessed him with.

The fame of the work spread rapidly and widely, and more than one tribe curiously watched its progress. It came to an end with a quickness which surprised all men, and there the fair structure stood,

towering aloft into the blue air, the greatest of all hall buildings, a gathering place
for happy men, defying destruction except
from the irresistible might of fire. It was
called Heorot—Hart-hall—because of the
noble crown of antlers which ran round
the eaves of the building,—and the opening banquet was an event long remembered in the land, from the bountiful
hospitality dispensed by the King and the
wealth of gifts, in rings and other precious
things, which he gave away with almost
reckless lavishness on this occasion.

II

GRENDEL

BUT there was one apart from all this joy who was consumed with malice and with hatred, who vowed to turn the joy into direst grief, the shouts of gladness into moans and wails, ere many days had come and gone. True, no human wight was he, but one of the unholy brood of monsters, accursed of God, who dwell in moors, fens, and swamps, remote from God-fearing men, ever bent on doing hell's work of harm and destruction—the unblest posterity (so wise men tell) of Cain, the first shedder of innocent blood.

To this Grendel, this outcast creature, dwelling in darkness, it was torture unbearable to hear the sounds of rejoicing day by day, as they came, borne by the wind to him, across the moor--the tender sighing of the harp, the ringing song of the minstrel.

Once, one skilled in holy song told of the creation of the world: how the Almighty made the earth, radiant with beauty, and the waters that encompass it, delighting in His work; and how He ordained the sun and the moon, for light to the dwellers on the earth, and made the woods beautiful with boughs and leaves; and how He put life into all the things that breathe and move.

Grimly the wicked one hearkened to the strain, which fed his unholy fury until it craved for slaughter, fell, immediate.

He set out that very night, as soon as darkness descended, made straight for the lofty hall. He did not much fear detection, for he knew that after such a carousal the warriors would be overcome with sleep. And truly, there they lay, in the hall itself, with their weapons by their side, yet helpless as unarmed women. He went, and, in their sleep, seized and killed thirty of the thanes; then hied him back to his moor with the war spoils, yelling with fierce joy.

Then was there a great cry in the grey morning. The voice of weeping was raised where but now the song of gladness had filled the air. Dazed and woe-begone, the King sat in his high place, and wept for his thanes. But when, the very next night, Grendel returned and committed even greater murder, and again and again after that, terror seized on them all. Men kept in close hiding from nightfall to break of day, then gradually left their own well-appointed homes, sleeping in barns or in the open, away from dwellings, wherever they thought they could best bestow themselves for safety; but naught availed to save. For twelve winters' space the baleful fiend warred single-handed against the Skyldings and their friends, till all the best houses stood deserted. Unbounded were the sorrows of that dreadful time, unspeakable the distress, and the fame thereof was carried to foreign lands in ballads and moving tales. Men dared not go within miles of the fated moor; so travel was stopped, tribute remained unpaid ; for the foul ruffian, a dark shadow of death prowled about and lay in wait. Of night he continually held the misty moors ; and no one knew what way the hellish birth moved in his rounds, for never was the monster seen of man. As to Heorot, the richly decorated hall, Grendel made that his headquarters, and occupied it every dark night. Only he was never able to come near the throne, because it stood on a consecrated spot, and was hallowed by priestly benison.

A great affliction, heart-breaking, was this that had come on the Skyldings and their friends. Many a time and oft did the best and wisest sit in council, seeking what were best be done in these awful straits. So sorely were they bested, that they forgot at times that they were Christians, and more than once craved help against the goblin visitant from the old heathen gods, vowing sacrifices at their secret shrines.

Thus was King Hrothgar perpetually tossed with the trouble of that time, and not all his wisdom availed to ward off the evil.

III

A FRIEND IN NEED

THERE lived at that time among the Goths, at the right hand of their King, Hygelac, a young thane, his cousin, of the name of Beowulf. He was, as his name betokened, one of the Skylding race, but only in the female line. Young as he was, he had won for himself a name of wide renown as a hero of high achievement and the mightiest among all the men of his time.

Now, this brave thane, in his distant home, heard of the misdeeds of Grendel, and his heart ached for the aged King, the evening of whose days was clouded over by such unheard-of tribulation. He made up his mind to help, and sued to King Hygelac for permission to undertake the venture with a few picked comrades. His friends of the King's council and board praised the gallant youth to the skies. They egged on his daring spirit, they took omens and consulted signs on his behalf ; but they did not begrudge him the adventure, wise men that they were, even though he was dear to them.

Beowulf ordered a good ship to be made ready for him, to take him over the road that swans travel.[1] He selected fourteen champions among the Goths, the keenest he could find, and went to sea with them, having made sure of a skilful, experienced pilot, who knew the shallows and the deeps. Like a bird the good ship, tight-timbered, slender-necked, sped before the wind, and made such way that on the next day already the eager voyagers saw land, gleaming cliffs, hills towering, headlands stretching out to sea : the passage was ended. Lightly the ethelings sprang ashore, made fast the ship, shook out their garments, saw to their arms, and gave thanks to God for that their seafaring had been easy.

---

[1] Literally true : the North Sea is the " path of the swans " and to this day wild swans abound on the coast of Norway.

IV

THE WARDEN

WHILE Beowulf and his friends were busy with their landing, thinking only of the work before them, the Skyldings' warden, he whose duty it was to guard the sea-cliffs and report any strangers that hove in sight, espied them from his high watch-place. Moved by curiosity as much as by duty, he rode down to the beach in great excitement, brandishing a powerful, huge lance, and demanded, in no gentle terms, to know the strangers' errand and nationality, before they could be allowed to proceed any farther into the land of the Danes.

Beowulf at once stepped forth and spoke up for all, with a dignity and courtesy which shamed the rude officer into more manly

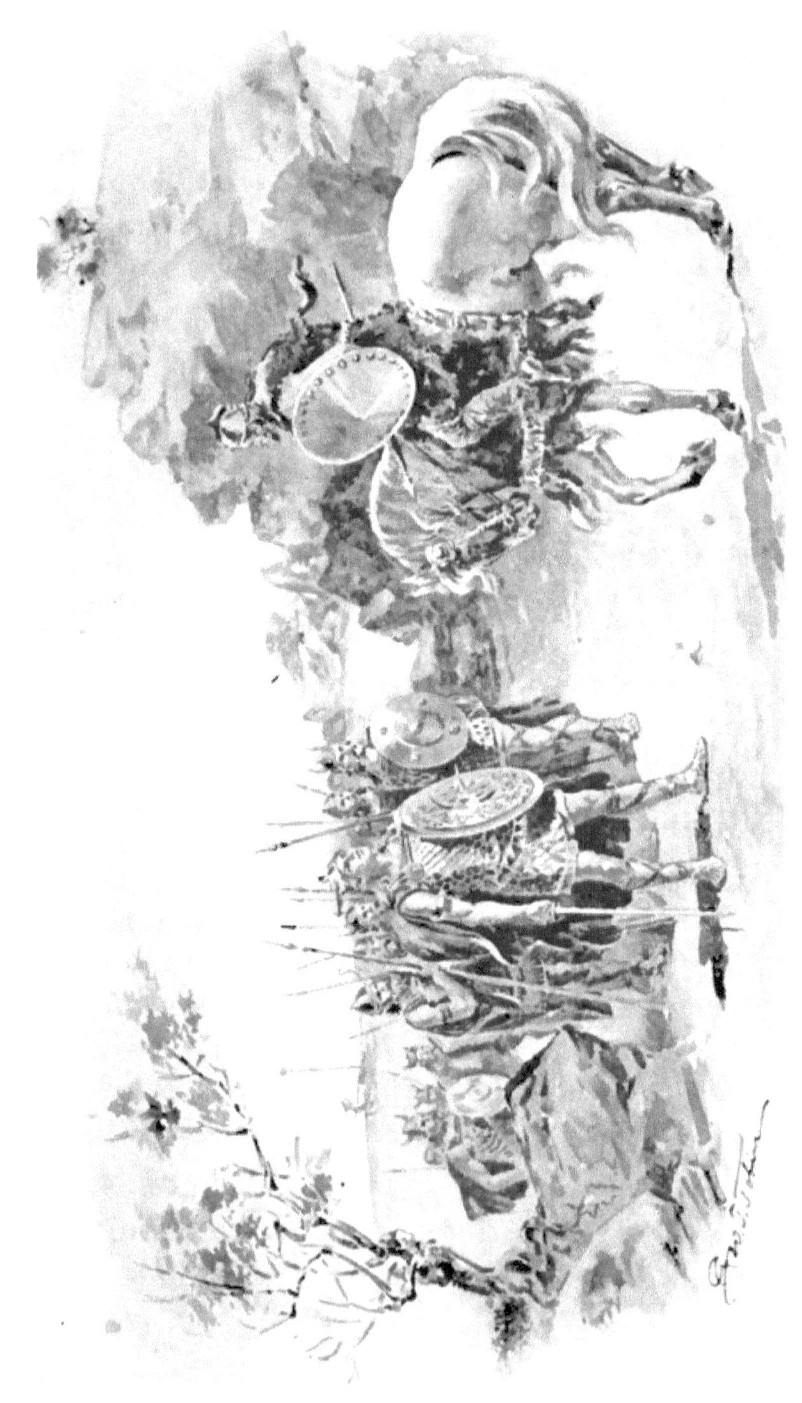

behaviour. He gave a full account of him-self, then concluded :

" We have come with friendly intent to visit thy lord. We have a great message to him ; nor is there, to my mind, any need to keep it dark. For it is no secret that the Skyldings are in great tribulation be-cause of a mysterious fiend, who has been vexing them for years with his nightly de-predations. Now I can teach Hrothgar the remedy, and bring back better times. This I say in all sincerity of heart."

To this speech the warden replied in greatly altered tones :

" I gather from what I hear that this is a friendly band come to visit the lord of the Skyldings. But it is a faithful ser-vant's part to question sharply and to gain certainty on all points before he commits his lord. Keep your arms and march on : I will guide you. Likewise will I com-mand my kinsmen thanes honourably to keep against every foe your vessel here on the beach."

Upon this invitation the troop gaily left their ship riding safely at her anchor, and eagerly pressed forward, until their eyes beheld the far-famed hall, Heorot the gold-roofed, most renowned of all mansions under the sky. Then the warden pointed with his hand to the road which led straight to it, wheeled round his horse, and spoke a parting word :

"It is time for me to go. May the all-wielding Father graciously keep you safe in adventures ! As for me, I must hie me back to the shore, to keep my watch against foes from the sea."

V

THE ARRIVAL

THE road was stone-paven, and so straight, there was no need of a guide. Beowulf and his band marched up to the Hall in grim, warlike guise, their burnished corslets shining, the iron rings of their mail shirts clanging loud. When they reached the mansion, the weary men set down their broad shields, leaning them against the wall, and seated themselves in silence on the bench before the entrance, after stacking their spears together, ready to their hand. Thus they waited in dignified silence for somebody to come from King Hrothgar and challenge them.

Very soon an officer appeared and put the customary questions, to which he added some respectful compliments :

"I am," he said, "Hrothgar's herald and esquire. Never saw I foreigners of loftier mien. I think that ye have come to visit Hrothgar, not from desperate fortunes, but bound on some high undertaking."

To which the proud leader replied with gallant bearing:

"We are Hygelac's own table-fellows. My name is Beowulf. I will myself expound mine errand to thy lord, if so he deign to admit us to his presence."

The officer, Wulfgar by name, hastened forthwith to where Hrothgar sat, old and hoary, and bent with grief, amid his despondent warriors, and not only told of the valiant guests from the land of the Goths and their petition, but advised him to give them a friendly reception. In the deep distress of these sorry times, it seemed as though any change must be for the better, and every stranger must bring hope.

The sad old King brightened at mention of Beowulf's name, whose father he had known in the dear departed days of golden youth, and whose own renown he pleasurably recalled.

" This son," he said, " I mind him well. I knew him when he was a page. He has grown into a valiant campaigner. It is said that he has thirty men's strength in his handgrip. Surely God of His grace hath sent him to us in our great need. Bid him and his men, one and all, into my presence straight, with every martial honour. Say to them, moreover, in words, that they are welcome."

VI

THE RECEPTION AND THE PLEDGE

WULFGAR, nothing loth, took the royal message to the waiting guests and ushered them into the royal presence in full warlike equipment, helm on head, sword on hip. Beowulf, tall and commanding, his corslet of cunningly linked mail shining as a network of lights, took his stand before the King, and, with firm eye and becoming assurance, spoke thus at length of what was nearest to his and the Danes' hearts :

"To Hrothgar hail ! I am King Hygelac's cousin-thane. Many a deed of daring was mine in youngsterhood. All that ye suffer here from Grendel became known to us in Gothland. Seafaring men told us how that this hall, this most princely fabric, stands useless and empty each night, as soon as the star of day is hidden from view. Then did my people, the wisest and best among them, urge me that I should visit thee, O royal Hrothgar. Because they knew the strength of my arm of their own knowledge : time and again they had seen me return from the field battered by foes, but never beaten ; five monsters I bound on land, and in the waves I slew many a nicor[1] in the night-time. And now I am bound to champion thy quarrel, O King, single-handed, against Grendel, the evil giant. But one petition I have, which thou, O Shelter of the Danes, wilt not refuse to one who is come from far to serve thee : it is that I may have the task alone—I and my band of earls—to purge Heorot. And as I have learnt that the terrible one, out of sheer boastfulness, despises the use of weapons, so I too will forego them, and bear not sword, nor spear, nor broad

[1] " Nicors " are mischievous water-sprites, who delight in making trouble for ships and sailors. The feminine in German is " Nixe," the beautiful water-maiden who lures mortals down into her watery abode.

shield to my battle with him ; but with handgrip alone will I meet him, foe to foe, and him of the two whom the Lord doometh, let grim Death take for his own.

" Should the doom fall upon me," Beowulf went on, " thou wilt not, O King, be put to the trouble of building a mound over my head. For if all tales of Grendel be true, he will bear away the gory corpse, to feast on it in his lonely moor. But this do thou for love of me ; send to Hygelac the matchless armour that protects my breast—it is a work of Weland, cunningest of smiths, and such are not made nowadays ; meet gift from a departing friend."

VII

THE FEAST

TO this speech, manly and heroic, Hroth-gar made reply in many words—for age is not sparing of its breath in words. He gave thanks to the God-sent young champion ; he went back to the deeds of his youth, in company with his brothers and many brave comrades long dead ; he dwelt on the horrors of these latter years. Then, at length bethinking himself that the wayfarers must be a-weary and a-hungered, he said to the chief :

" But now sit thee down to the banquet with thy fellows, and merrily share the feast as the spirit moves thee."

A table was promptly cleared for the Goths. Thither they went, and sat in the pride of their strength. A thane at-

tended to their wants, going from one to
the other with a mighty ale-can of handsome workmanship. Again and again he
poured out the golden ale. At times a
minstrel's voice rose in Heorot, ringing
and clear, and there was right brave merriment and good-will in this mixed company
of Goths and Danes.

Yet was there one eye that gleamed
not with merriment and good-will, one head
that hatched no friendly thoughts, because
the heart swelled with malice and envy.
Unferth it was, the King's own story-teller,
who sat at his feet, to be ready at all times
to amuse him. He broached a quarrel-
some theme—an adventure in Beowulf's
early youth, the only contest in his record
the issue of which, though hard fought,
might be called doubtful. For this Unferth was an envious wight, whose soul
grudged that any man should achieve
greater things than himself.

" Art thou not," he began tauntingly,
" that same Beowulf who strove with Breca
on open sea in a swimming match, in which
ye both wantonly exposed your lives, and

no man, either friend or foe, could turn
you from the foolish venture? A se'n-
night ye twain toiled in the realm of the
waters, and, if I err not, he outdid thee
in swimming, for he had greater strength.
Wherefore I fear me much thou mayest
meet with sorry luck if thou darest to
bide here for Grendel for the space of a
whole night."

Beowulf, though angered, controlled his
temper and replied with great coolness:

"Big things are these, friend Unferth,
which thou hast spoken; evidently, good
ale has loosened thy wits. Yes,—Breca
and I used to talk between ourselves when
we were pages, and brag each of his prowess, being but youngsters, and so we made
up the foolish match between us, and having made it, we stuck to it. Drawn sword
in hand we went into the water: we meant
to guard ourselves against sea-monsters
and water-sprites. Five nights we kept
close together, then the flood parted us.
It was a dark night, freezing cold, and a
fierce wind from the north came dead
against us, the waves running rough and

high. One spotty monster dragged me to the bottom ; but I did not lose my grip on my sword and despatched the mighty sea-brute. I know not how many more I fought and killed : it was a grewsome night. At last, light broke in the east, and the waves grew calmer, so I could see the headlands, and the sea cast me up on the shore. I escaped with my life, though worn and spent, and never heard I of harder fight, or of man sorer distressed. Anyhow, it was my good luck that I slew with the sword nine nicors. So many less were left to play havoc with seafaring ships. Therefore, methinks I may rightly claim that I have proved more sea-prowess, endured more buffetings from waves, than any other man."

Thus Beowulf told of his youthful prank. Then turning upon Unferth with flashing eye and clouded brow—

"Of a sooth," he cried, "I say to thee, Unferth, that never had Grendel, the foul ruffian, made up such a tale of horrors, wrought such disgrace in Heorot, if thy spirit were as high as thou wouldst claim for thyself. But he has found out that he has not much to fear from the mighty Danes ; so he takes blackmail, and slaughters and feasts at his ease. But now the Goth shall ere long show him another kind of spirit, and when the light of another day rises over the world, then shall all who choose walk proudly into the hall, with head erect."

This speech, so brave and cheery, gladdened the old King's heart, and even the Danes applauded it, although it held a bitter sting : they took it as a well-deserved hit at the unmannerly Unferth. So laughter greeted Beowulf's words, music sounded again, jolly drinking-songs filled the hall ; and none seemed to remember—although at heart none forgot it—that night was coming on, and what it was to bring.

And now, behold ! Hrothgar's royal consort, Queen Wealhtheow, well versed in ceremonies and courtly lore, entered the hall, resplendent in cloth of gold, to honour her husband's guests with a gracious word and a draught of sweet

mead from her own royal hands. Her
stately greeting took in all the men in the
hall ; then she presented the beaker with
graceful obeisance to her lord, wishing
him blithe at the banquet, and happy in
his liegemen's love. Then she went the
round of the hall, to elder and younger,
and to each she handed the jewelled cup,
until she came to where Beowulf was
sitting among the young ethelings. With
befitting dignity she greeted the leader of
the Goths, as he stood before her, thanking God with wise choice of words that her
heart's desire had come to pass. He,
the hero of many battles, took the beaker
from her hand, and, ere he drained it,
repeated his solemn pledge :

" When I went on board and sat in my
ship, as she sped over the waters, with
this my chosen band, I vowed I would
work out the deliverance of your people.
I am bound as an earl to fulfil my vow, or
in this hall to meet my death to-night."

He quaffed the mead, and she, the
noble lady, inclined her diademed head
as she took from him the cup, for his

QUEEN WEALHTHEOW PLEDGES BEOWULF.

words were well to her liking. Then slowly, with trailing robes, she walked to the head of the hall, to sit by her lord.

For some time yet the banqueting went on as merrily as ever,—until the daylight began to wane, when suddenly song and laughter died on the revellers' lips, and King Hrothgar bethought himself that it was time to retire, for he knew that the monster came forth when shrouding night decends and the creatures of darkness go stalking abroad. In silence all the company arose.

Hrothgar greeted Beowulf and spoke solemn words :

" Never before, since my hand lifted shield, did I entrust the Guard-house of the Danes to any man,—never but now to thee. Have and hold the sacred house against the foe. Be watchful, valiant, and may victory wait on thee! No wish of thine shall go unfulfilled if thou dost perform the great work and livest to tell it."

Thus spoke Hrothgar the Skylding, and gravely departed from the hall, with his Queen, followed by his men.

VIII

THE COMBAT

SILENTLY Beowulf looked after the Danes; silently he began to divest himself of his armour, mindful of his vow to fight the goblin bare-handed. He laid off his shining mail, his helmet and his sword of choicest steel, and gave them in charge to his esquire; then he stretched himself on the floor and laid his cheek on a pillow. For the hall had meanwhile been promptly cleared of tables and benches, which were pushed against the walls, and couches of soft pelts and rugs were spread on the floor. His comrades did likewise. Not that rest came to any of them at first; for not one thought in his heart he should ever again see his own folk, his native land, the castle where he was nurtured. But even as they kept turning these things over in their minds, their limbs relaxed, their lids grew heavy with very weariness, and—they slept. All slept, but one,—and he lay quite still, straining his ear to listen and his eye to peer through the dim night.

And hark! tramp, tramp, he came marching from the moor,—Grendel, the God-sent scourge. Straight for the hall he made through the gloom : it was not the first time he visited Hrothgar's homestead ; but never had he met such a welcome as now awaited him there.

He came carelessly along, as one assured of his entertainment. The door, though fastened with bars of wrought iron, sprang open at his touch. Quickly he stepped across the flagged floor, big with rage, with eyes ablaze. Suddenly he perceived the troop of strange warriors, lying close together, asleep. He laughed aloud. He gloated as he stood over them, and thought that, ere day came, the life of each of them should have been wrenched from the body, since luck had sent him such a treat.

Beowulf curbed his rage to watch the fell ruffian and see how he meant to proceed. The delay was not long: Grendel quickly, at one grab, seized a sleeping warrior, tore him up, crunched the bony frame, drank the blood from the veins, swallowed the flesh in huge morsels; in a trice he had devoured the lifeless body, feet, hands, and all. Then he stepped forward to where the hero lay, and reached out a hand to seize him on his bed—but suddenly felt his arm held tight in such a grip as he had never met with from any man in all the world. He knew at once that he was in an evil plight—in mortal fear he strove to wrench himself free and flee. This was not the entertainment he had been wont to meet there in bygone days.

Now all were awake, and the hall was in an uproar. And over at the castle, a deadly panic came over all the Danes, noble or simple, brave men as they were. Furious were both the maddened champions; the hall resounded with their wrestling. It was a great wonder the building did not fall to the ground; only that it was inwardly and outwardly made strong with iron stanchions, with such masterly skill. In this night of terror it made good the Danes' boast that no mortal force short of fire would ever be able to wreck it.

The noise rose high, with increasing violence. The Danes outside were numb with horror at the unearthly shrieks and dismal howlings of the God-forsaken fiend. Many an earl of Beowulf's unsheathed and plunged into the fight; they knew not that they could not help their leader, much as they desired it, for that no choicest blade on earth could touch that destroyer, because he had secured himself by spells and incantations against weapons of all kinds. But he was not proof against human heroic might, and from that he now got his death-wound, as Beowulf, with a desperate grip and tug, wrenched his arm off from the shoulder. With a terrific yell, which told the listening Danes that the dire struggle was ended, and victory won by their champion, Grendel fled to the coverts of the fen : well he knew that the number of his days was full.

Thus was the valiant champion's pledge redeemed ; thus was Heorot purged.   The leader of the Goths had made good his vaunt, and, in token thereof, he hung up Grendel's hand, arm, and shoulder—grim trophy !—under the gabled roof.

IX

REJOICINGS AND THANKSGIVINGS

EARLY in the morning there was a great gathering about the hall. Chieftains came from far and near, to hear the marvellous tale, to gaze at the loathsome prodigy. Then they took up the vanquished monster's bloody trail, and followed it to the Nicors' Mere, whither, death-doomed and fugitive, he had betaken himself to die. There was the face of the lake surging with blood, the gruesome plash of waves all turbid with reeking gore. There he had yielded up his heathen soul, there pale-faced Hela, the dread queen and guardian of the heathen dead, received it.

After surveying the uncanny spot, they rode home from the Mere in high glee, as from a pleasure-trip. Now and then one and the other loosened their nags for a gallop, to run a match where the turf looked smooth and inviting. Then again a thane of the King's, his mind full of ballads, stored with old-world tales, began to compose Beowulf's adventure into a story on the spot, to be sung later at the feast, to the sweet-stringed harp. Or yet another compared him to Siegfried, the Dragon-slayer, the greatest hero of all North countries.

Thus, alternately racing and talking and singing, they rode joyously back to the hall, and when they reached there, the sun was already high in the sky, and crowds were still flocking to Heorot; and the King himself, with the Queen and with a gorgeous following of lords and ladies, was coming the short way from his palace to view his enemy's monstrous arm and hand hanging from the gold-glittering roof.

Hrothgar was very different this sunny morning from the bent and sorrow-stricken old man who greeted Beowulf the night before as his last hope on earth. Right royal he looked now in his rich

robes as he walked along with head erect
and firm step, and clear, glad eye. He
stood awhile, gazing silently on the horrible hand, with fiendish fingers, and nails
straight and sharp like steel spikes,—then
devoutly raised his voice :

" For this sight thanks be given the
Almighty ! It was but now that I
thought I should never see an end of all
my woes—and now a lad, through the
might of God, has achieved the deed
which we, with all our wisdom, were unable to accomplish. Now I will heartily
love thee, Beowulf, thou most excellent
youth ! From this day forth shalt thou
be to me as my son ; thou shalt have
nothing to wish for in the world so far as
I have power. Full oft have I, for far
less service, decreed great guerdons from
my treasury. May the Almighty reward
thee always, as He hath just done !"

Beowulf accepted these thanks and
praises with most becoming modesty.
Indeed, he rather apologised for having
let the enemy escape him ; " for," he said,
" I would have liked vastly better to show

thee his very self, instead of only his arm
and hand."

Men, in those days, were not, as a rule,
shy of boasting of their valorous deeds
and making the most of them. Therefore
the young hero's quiet bearing won him
still heartier admiration and louder ap-
plause. One man alone in all that joy-
ous crowd kept silent and to himself—and
that was Unferth, the story-teller, who had
given vent so freely to his envious malice
at the feast. He dared not now either
brag of his own doings, or belittle Beowulf's exploit, and so held his peace.
But in his heart, alone of all men, he
grudged him his triumph.

X

HEOROT RESTORED—FEASTING AND GIFTS

AND now orders were given that Heorot should be promptly swept, cleansed, and decorated; men and women trooped in in great numbers to do the work. No light work it was, for the whole interior of the building was nearly demolished; in fact, the roof alone escaped quite unhurt. Substantial repairs, of course, would take time; but the hall must be garnished and made ready for that day's banquet. So they hid the walls with brocaded tapestries which delighted the eye with their pictured stories.

When the time came, King Hrothgar walked to the Hall, for he intended to

share the entire feast from beginning to
end.   And never did a braver throng of
revellers muster more merrily around the
feast-giver.

The first beaker of sweet mead the
King drank to Beowulf, and at the same
time presented him with a complete suit
of preciously-wrought, gold-adorned, armour—helmet, coat of mail, and heavy
battle-sword, all from the royal treasury.
Then, at a sign from the King, eight beautiful horses, with cheekplates of gold, were
led into the hall.   One of them was gaily
caparisoned and bore the King's own favourite saddle, all decorated with silver.
Horse and saddle were well known to all
present, having been seen often and often
both at knightly games and in the field,
where foemen fell before the royal rider
both in play and in deadly earnest.   Arms
and horses the King bade the young hero
have for his own, and enjoy them well.

Moreover, each one of those who had
made the voyage with Beowulf received
some precious gift, some old heirloom.
As for the comrade whom Grendel had

so atrociously killed and devoured, King Hrothgar gave order that gold should be brought from his treasury, to make good his loss to his people.

And now the King called aloud for music and song. The harp was struck and Hrothgar's minstrel recited a ballad, often heard, but always a favourite, a lay of an old feud and vengeance, which made the revellers realise the more joyfully their deliverance from the tribute of blood which, through so many years, they had unwillingly paid.

The merriment ran high, and high rose the sounds of revelry as the attendants served the wine out of curious flagons. When suddenly there was a pause : Queen Wealhtheow came forward, wearing right nobly her golden diadem, and, as the day before, stood before her lord, and spoke :

"Receive this beaker, King of the Danes ! Be merry thyself, and gladden those around thee with gifts and gracious words. For now, far and near, thou hast peace. Heorot is purged and is once more the most splendid of banqueting-halls. Dispense, then, thy bounties while thou mayest, and to thy children peacefully leave folk and realm when thy time comes to pass into eternity."

She turned then towards the bench where her young sons sat. And there, by the two brothers, Beowulf modestly sat among the youth of the land, separate from the elders and mighty men. To him the Queen offered the beaker, with friendly words, inviting him to drink, then presented him with her own special gifts: a rich mantle, armlets of twisted gold, and rings, and—crowning gift of all —a jewelled carcanet, the most gorgeous piece of jeweller's work ever seen under the sun.

"Wear this collar, Beowulf, beloved youth," the Queen said, "and make use of this mantle—stately possessions both— Prosper well, win more and more fame by thy valour, and to these my boys be true friend and kind adviser. Thou hast done that which will make thee the theme of minstrels' song, far and near, for all time. Be then, whilst thou livest, a happy prince, and loyal to my sons in word and deed. For such is the manner of our land : here is each warrior to other true, loyal to their chief ; the thanes obedient, the people willing. And now, I bid ye all—be merry ! "

With that she walked to her chair, and music once more filled the hall, and wine flowed freely. No thought was there of evil to come, only of the evil from which they deemed that they were freed forever : for who ever hears the fiat of destiny as it goes forth ? . . . And so the evening came, and Hrothgar betook him to his rest.

Silence fell upon Heorot ; the festive sounds died out. For the first time in many years, the hall was not deserted for the night ; the ethelings stayed to guard it as they had often done in earlier times. The benches were cleared away against the walls ; beds and bolsters were laid in rows upon the floor, and the revellers laid themselves down to rest, happy and at peace. Yet did one among them lie down that night a doomed man, and knew it not.

At their heads they set up their bright
bucklers; on the benches, plain in sight,
lay each etheling's helmet and mail-shirt,
and against them stood the strong-shafted
lances.   For such was their custom—to
be at all times ready for war, whether at
home or in the field, wherever their liege
lord might have need of their services.
Truly a brave and noble people!

LAY II

GRENDEL'S MOTHER

I

THE AVENGER

SO they sank down to sleep. One there was who sorely paid for that night's rest. For ere morning it was found that Grendel had left an avenger—his mother, the Mere-wife, loathsome beldame, a creature that had to dwell in the dreariness of marshes and cold streams, like all the rest of Cain's murderous, outlawed brood. That very night the hag, on bloody vengeance bent, betook herself to Heorot, where the Danes slept careless, all unconscious. Who shall paint their horror and dismay when the goblin-wife suddenly burst into their midst? Swords were drawn and bucklers raised, but there was no time to think of helmet or mail-shirt.

The hag was in a hurry; finding herself discovered, all she thought of was to get away with her life. So she quickly snatched up one of the ethelings at random, and gripping him tight, made for the fen. That man was Hrothgar's dearest comrade, most constant companion— sad end for an illustrious warrior! But hurried as she was, the hag managed to carry away with her Grendel's arm and hand. A great cry went up from Heorot, and reached the aged King, who was startled out of his sleep by the news that the old horror was revived, and that the man dearest to his heart was dead.

Beowulf was not there. No one thought that his prowess should be needed again; so, as he was in want of rest after his last night's exertions, he and his companions had been assigned a lodging at some distance, and they knew nothing of what had happened. Bright and early, he and his little band, rested, cheery, marched to the palace, straight to the King's apartment, the floor-timbers resounding under their tread, and, courteously accosting him, enquired if, according to their sincere wish, he had had a restful night.

Great was their astonishment to find the King more deeply dejected than ever, the tears coursing down his withered cheeks, and to hear his heart-broken answer:

"Speak not of rest to me! New grief has come over the Danes. Æschere is dead, my friend and counsellor, my trusty body-squire, who has stood with me, shoulder to shoulder, in battle, a hundred times. In Heorot has he met his death at the hands of another raging fiend. Yesternight didst thou overcome Grendel in deadly fight, and now his mother comes to avenge her kin! I know not in what direction she took her way, but her tracks will show. I will be bound they lead us no farther than the Mere, a few miles from here—an uncanny water—wolf-crags, windy bluffs, woods with gnarled, intertwined roots overhang it. A precipitous mountain waterfall vanishes into the earth, and flows on, an underground river. And on the Mere itself, every night, a fearful portent may be seen : fire playing on the water. The man liveth not who knows the depth of that mere. The antlered hart, as he makes for the wood coverts, harried by hounds, will sooner give up life on the bank, than plunge his head into the unhallowed flood. Now it is once more to thee alone that we look for counsel! Thou knowest not yet the dreadful haunt—go seek it if thou dare! I will reward thee with treasure to thy heart's content, if so thou comest away alive."

Beowulf answered straightway, and his brave words fell like balm on Hrothgar's dejected spirits :

"Cease sorrowing, wise sire! Avenging a friend is better than mourning for him. Arouse thee! let us promptly set out to find the trail of this new terror. I vow to thee she shall not escape ; neither in the bowels of the earth, nor in the haunted woods, nor in ocean's depth—go where she will! Have patience but this one day, and all thy woes shall end."

II

THE MERE

UP sprang then the aged King, thanking God for the hero's words, which
filled him with new vigour. He mounted
his charger, a stately high-stepper with
wavy, flowing mane, and rode forth with
Beowulf and the mixed band of Danes and
Goths, the foot-force of shield-bearing men
marching behind. The track lay broad
and plain over the ground, down the
slope—straight across the murky moor.

Lightly did Beowulf step over steep
stone-banks, narrow gullies, lonesome,
untravelled paths, sheer bluffs, under many
of which were deep caverns, the dwelling-
place of nicors. With a few tried men
he went forward, exploring the ground,
until all of a sudden he perceived the

gloomy trees overhanging the grisly rock of which Hrothgar had spoken—a cheerless wood; beneath it a standing water, dreary and troubled. The whole scene was so desolate and eerie that it made the Danes shudder; horror seized them as they looked, for on that cliff they came on the head of Æschere in a pool of blood.

The horn sounded from time to time a spirited blast to keep them together. But they had little wish to stray. They all sat down on the ground, terrified, yet curious for the weird sights of the Mere: they saw gliding along the water many shapes of serpent kind, monstrous sea-snakes at their swimming gambols; likewise nicors lying lazily on the jutting slopes,—the water-goblins which often, of an early morning, churn up the waves to make disastrous sailing for voyagers,—dragons, and other strange beasts tumbled about, then hurried away with eye of spite and body swelling with rage at being disturbed by the clarion's clang and the intrusion of men. Beowulf, with an arrow from his bow, picked off one of the monsters, which was swiftly pulled out on land; his swimming days were over, his tricks ended.

But this was play. The business of the day was now to come, and Beowulf began to prepare for it. Piece by piece he donned his princely armour, which was to stand the novel test of deadly battle in the waters of the unholy lake. Most anxiously did his friends, both Danes and Goths, watch and assist him as he silently armed, with brow and mouth firmly set under the helmet, for well they knew that the contest he was now going to engage in was far more dangerous than that in which he had but lately ventured life and limb. Even Unferth, the unmannerly, forgot what he had recently uttered when flushed with ale—or perchance he wished to atone for past ill-will by present service. Enough, he pressed to Beowulf's side, and placed in his hand a wonderful sword, an old heirloom of his house, most highly prized of all his possessions. That precious blade, like other famed swords belonging to mighty heroes, had a name of its own, like a human friend: it was called Hrunting. The edge of the blade was iron, welded onto the brass, mottled with poison, and hardened in the gore of many battles. Never had it proved false to him who wielded it; this was not the first time that heroic work had been required of it.

III

UNDER THE WATERS

AND now Beowulf stood armed, and ready for the fray. But before he went whence he might not come back, he turned to King Hrothgar and once again repeated the request he had made before he remained in Heorot to await the coming of Grendel:

"See now, O wise King, I am ready to start. Bethink thee of what we lately talked of: that, should I lose my life in thy service, thou shouldst, after my death, fulfil my wishes even as my own father would. They are but few and easily remembered: be thou friend and protector to my thanes when I am gone, and send the presents thou hast given me to Hygelac; so will he see for himself that I had found a bountiful friend.   And let Unferth keep my own heirloom, my curiously damaskeened sword, Hardedge.   With Hrunting I will either achieve renown or find my death."

He said, and, waiting for no answer, leaped from the bluff—the eddying flood engulfed him.   So deep was the mere, that it took some time before, sinking, he reached the bottom.

Soon the grim creature that for a hundred seasons had kept house in the watery realm perceived that one of the children of men was coming from above, exploring the goblins' home.   She made a grab at him and clutched him in her grisly talons, but could not pierce the well-knit ring mail which fenced him around.   But she bore him to her mansion at the bottom of the lake, so swiftly that, although his heart did not fail, he was powerless to use his weapons, the more that countless water-beasts harassed him in swimming, battering at him with tusk and claw.

At length the earl felt the grip loosened on him, and as he hurriedly cast his eye

BEOWULF AND THE OLD WIFE OF THE MERE.

around, he perceived that he was in a vast hall, high-roofed, and protected from the water on all sides; it was light, too, with an eerie, bright lustre, something like firelight. But the hero had no time for wonder or exploring; for before him stood the grim she-wolf of the abyss, and it behoved him to be quick in attack. Grasping Hrunting, he whirled it around her head; but when it descended to strike, he found, to his dismay, that the edge did not bite; for the first time the costly blade failed the master at his need. With prompt decision he angrily flung it away, and once again trusting wholly to his own strength, seized the hag by the shoulder, and swayed her so violently in his rage that she sank to the pavement. She swiftly repaid him and closed in upon him, crushing the wind out of his body, so that he, fearless as he was, staggered from sheer breathlessness and fell prostrate. Then the hag sat upon his back and drew her broad knife, and her goblin son would have been avenged then and there, but that Beowulf's mail-shirt was proof against point and edge, which gave him time for a last mighty effort to throw off the hindering weight,—and presently he stood once more erect on his feet.

Still, even then his life might have been forfeit in the unequal combat, had he not chanced to espy among the armour lying scattered about the hall, an old cutlass of huge size and strength of blade, larger than an ordinary man could have carried, let alone used in battle,—the handiwork of giants. On this Beowulf blindly seized— beside himself, despairing of his life—and struck in his fury; the blow caught the beldame in the neck, severed the bone, she dropped on the pavement,—the work was done.

He was alone. He now had leisure to scan the apartment with his eye; he slowly walked all round it, along by the wall, the magic weapon swung aloft by the hilt, for fear of surprises. Suddenly, he came upon a hideous object—Grendel, bereft of life, lying where he fell, as he reached his lake home on that fatal night. The hero's blood boiled at the sight; he at once decided he would bring back to the upper world a better trophy than a hand and arm : so, raising high the cutlass, he struck off the head.

Then, before his eyes, there came to pass a thing whereat he marvelled much ; no sooner had the blade touched the monster's black gore, than it began to melt away, even as ice when the spring breathes upon it, dissolving the fetters of the torrent ; and even as he looked, it melted all to naught, down to the hilt in his hand—so venomous and consuming had been the goblin's life-blood !

There were many rare arms and trinkets in that wondrous water hall ; but Beowulf only glanced at them and would not burden himself with aught save the head, and the hilt of the burned-up cutlass, which he wanted to show and keep as a curiosity. Nor would he leave Hrunting below, since the good sword did not belong to him.

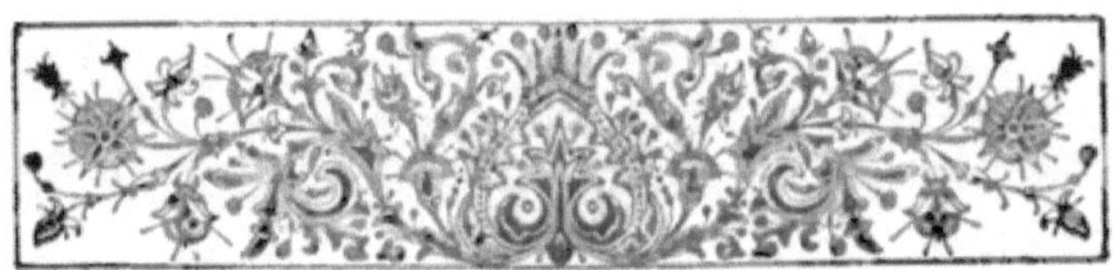

IV

THE RETURN

MEANWHILE the hours waxed long to the watchers above. Hrothgar and his men sat in the same spot still, intently gazing on the water. The old men with grizzled locks spoke together in low tones about the brave etheling, how they did not expect that he should ever come back to them; and when they saw the waves splashing turbid and tinged with blood, most of them decided that the she-wolf of the Mere had torn him to pieces.

It was the ninth hour of the day. The impetuous Danes gave him up for lost and quitted the bluff; King Hrothgar followed them with heavy heart. They did not doubt but that they had lost their hero-friend, and the nightly ravages would commence again. But the Goths would not go. Sick at heart they sat on, and gazed upon the dreadful pool. They did not expect to ever again get sight of their lord and captain in the body, yet they kept on wishing, and secretly hoping : for was he not greater and braver than all other men ? No other would have even dreamed of plunging into such an adventure.

And lo ! what was that ? something in the distance, moving on the water ! Water-beast it could not be, for they had all slunk away when man and goblin-wife met, and kept in hiding, waiting for the end. It was—yes, it was the leader ! Soon they could see him plainly, as he came swimming bravely along. He shouted to them. They answered with a cry which must have been heard half-way to Heorot. Then he came to land, exulting in his lake spoils. His faithful thanes ran to meet him, thanking God that they had him back, whole and sound. They pressed around, vieing who should relieve him of his helmet, his mail-shirt. From the moment he stepped on land, the Mere sullenly subsided, grey and heavy, leaden water under leaden sky.

And now Beowulf and his band prepared to retrace their steps, for they had quite a long way to march across country and along the public highways. So they formed into a triumphal procession, to bear away Grendel's head from the Mere-cliff : it took four of the lusty and stalwart fellows to carry it on a pole, and the burden taxed their strength to the utmost ; so that, when they reached the great hall, gold-glittering in the sunshine, they were glad to lay it down on the ground. Then others of their comrades took it up and carried it by the hair into the midst of the assembled Danes. Their captain was just greeting the King, but all sprang to their feet ; even to Hrothgar and the Queen, startled out of ceremony by the unexpected sight of the horrible object.

V

LAST WORDS

WHEN some sort of order had been restored, Beowulf, with his wonted modest dignity, gave the King a brief account of his last and most deadly encounter :

" Lo and behold! to thee, O Lord of the Skyldings, we have joyfully brought these Mere-spoils that thou lookest on, in token that what we came to do is done. Not easily did I come out of it with life. In the battle under water well-nigh had the struggle gone against me, only that God shielded me. I could not, in the final test, accomplish aught with Hrunting, though it be a good weapon, too. But the Ruler of men directed my eye to the wall, where it was caught by the gleam of an old sword of huge size, whereat I grasped, blindly. Thus oftenest hath He guided men when they have no other friend. With that sword—occasion favouring me,—I smote the keepers of the Mere-house, the living and the dead. So hot and poisonous was that accursed blood, that it consumed the blade, as thou canst see. I brought away the hilt as a trophy. And now that I have avenged the long agonies of the Danes as was meet, I promise thee that thou mayest sleep henceforth in Heorot free from care ; and so may every one of the thanes, old and young, and thou needest not fear for them any kind of danger, as thou didst so long."

The oldest and wisest among the warriors marvelled much to hear so wise a speech from lips so young. That in the heat of victory, hard-won, single-handed, the noble champion should remember to give thanks where alone man's thanks are due, and should generously share the credit with his comrades, pleased King Hrothgar greatly. With kindly smile he took the gilded, bladeless hilt into his hand and examined it intently. It was well worth the study, this relic of heathen times immemorial, the workmanship of giants. The mystic smiths had graven much ancient lore on it in quaint old characters, looking like small staves oddly thrown together, and long held sacred by learned men, who called them " Runes." Hrothgar, who, though himself a fervent Christian, was well versed in the ancient heathen lore of his people, easily read the storied gold of the hilt. Upon it was written the history of the primeval quarrel between the bright, beneficent gods and the perverse race of giants, and of the war between them, in which the wicked giants did their worst, by force and wile, to destroy the beautiful world, the creation of the gods, until the latter sent a great flood, and the giant's brood perished. Likewise was it set down in runes on a part of the mounting, for whom that sword had first been worked with its dragon ornament.

When he had examined the curious relic

at his leisure, King Hrothgar returned it
to the youth, and bending on him his
kindest glance, he spoke to him,—while
all around respectfully held their peace,—
out of the fulness of his heart and of his
long-hoarded wisdom, such words as only
a father speaks to a well-beloved son, when
he sends him forth to fare for himself in
the wide and dangerous world. For well
he knew that the hero, his mission done,
would leave him very soon, to continue
his adventurous career, wherever it might
call him, and his heart ached to let him
go ; he would fain have warned him of all
that might befall him on his way, and
given him his own treasure of experience
to guide and to shield him,—above all
against the dangers and snares of his own
untamed nature.

"Thy fame, friend Beowulf," the King
began, "will spread after this to every
land, over every nation. Thou dost withal
carry thy prowess modestly, with discretion of mind. Thou art fated to prove
a comfort sure and lasting to thy men, a
help to mankind."

Here the King recalled, as a warning example, the fate of Heremod, the bad king, who had lost the people's hearts through his arrogance and cruelty, and whom his (Hrothgar's), own ancestor, Skyld of the Sheaf, had displaced.

"Do thou take warning by that!" he continued. "It is for thy benefit that I, being old in years and experience, have told this tale. For, how many a time do we not see a man of noble race who dwelleth in prosperity, with nothing to annoy him, no care nor quarrel on any side, but all the world seems to move to his mind. Until, at length, within the man himself something of arrogancy grows and develops. Then sleepeth the heavenly guardian, the soul's keeper; the foe is very near, and the man yields to the crooked counsels of the accursed spirit; he fancies that all is too little that he has so long enjoyed; he grows covetous and malignant, and grudges to share his wealth with his friends. He too lightly considers how that it was God the Dispenser who placed him in his post of dignity. And then the end comes ; another fills his room who makes better use of his wealth—he is forgotten. Beware of such a fall, Beowulf, beloved youth, and choose for thyself the better course. Now is thy strength in full bloom for a while. Soon it may betide that sickness or the sword will bereave thee of it; fire or flood, stab of knife, or flight of spear—anything at any time may mar and darken all, and Death subdue thee, leader of men though thou art! Look at me: did I not for fifty years reign prosperously over the Danes, and by valour make them secure against many a nation, insomuch that I dreaded no rival under the circuit of the sky? Yet how suddenly a change came over all that ; here in my own hall, the abominable Grendel bearded and despoiled me, and for years my heart carried its load of grief. Thanks, therefore, be to the Eternal Ruler for what I have lived to see—that I, the old tribulation past, with mine own eyes should gaze upon yon severed head !—And now go, sit thee down, share the festive joy, crowned with the honours of war.

To-morrow we must yet have many dealings together."

Beowulf had listened with beseeming earnestness and reverence, nor did the aged king's wise instruction fall on barren soil. But he was very tired : so he moved briskly off and sat down, nothing loth, on one of the benches. Then the tables were cleared and re-spread, and a fair, fresh banquet served.

Not till the night's dim covering began to descend over the light-hearted revellers did the venerable Skylding arise and give the signal for bed. After him the elders. Vastly well did the hero of the day like the thought of repose—he had enough of adventure for a while! He was marshalled to his room with much ceremony by a chamberlain, who supplied him with all things needful for a luxurious night's rest. And he slept! slept till the black raven announced heaven's glory with blithe heart, and the light drove the shadows away, and fiends that prowl of nights scampered off and hid.

When he came forth from his sleeping·

chamber, he found his comrades all ready for the voyage. They were impatient to take ship for home.

Beowulf bade courteous farewell to his Danish friends, and when the turn of Unferth came, he returned Hrunting to him with hearty thanks for the loan; with never a word did he blame the blade that had played him false, but on the contrary praised it for a good sword, a good friend in war. Thus are high-souled men ever courteous and mindful of other men's feelings.

VI

HOMEWARD BOUND

ONLY when the departing warriors were fully equipped and ready to start, did Beowulf approach the raised platform where Hrothgar sat, to take loving leave of him.

" Now," he began, "we sea-voyagers have come to say that we purpose this very day to return to Hygelac. Here we have been well entertained, and thou hast been to us very generous. If I therefore may in any way be of use to thee, even though it require labour beyond what I have yet done, I shall be forthwith on hand. If they bring me word across the seas that thou art hard pressed by neighbours, I will at once bring thee a thousand thanes to help. And Hygelac, I know.

albeit young in years, will bear me out in this, and send me over with a forest of spears, shouldst thou have need of them."

The old King was deeply moved as he made answer :

" The All-wise Lord himself, puts such thoughts into thy mind. Never have I heard one so young in years discourse such sweet and reasonable speech. I think it very likely that, should sickness or iron take thy chief from this life, the seafaring Goths will find no better man than thyself to be their king. Thou hast my best wishes, beloved Beowulf, for I like thee more and more. Thou hast done that which will make the Danes and the Goths friends forevermore. While I rule this realm, the two nations shall have all things in common, and ships shall bring back and forward, not men armed for war, but presents and tokens of love."

King Hrothgar rose from his chair of state and pressed on his young friend twelve more priceless jewels, bidding him go with God and visit his people, but come back again soon. He clasped him by the neck, tears coursing down his cheeks into his long grey beard. To him the youth was so dear that he could not restrain the passion of his sorrow at parting from him, for, in spite of his cheery words, there was that in his breast which warned him that they two were not to meet again.

Beowulf, being young, was not much disturbed by forebodings, and when he left the hall, his foot trod the grassy earth with the firm step of conscious power. As he and his gallant troop neared the water, where their well-guarded ship awaited them, the coast-warden marked their approach, as he had done at their coming; but there was no suspicion now in his mind or manner, as he hailed them from his high peak and rode down swiftly towards them. The beach was all alive as the Goths proceeded, with right good will, to load the good ship with the war harness, the horses, and all the treasures from Hrothgar's hoard. Winds and waves seemed to favour their impatience, and sail and oars carried them smoothly over the foamy swell, till they were able to espy the familiar cliffs and headlands of the Gothic shore. And now the keel grated on the sand, the wind pushing from behind—she was on land.

The warden was ready to receive the seafarers at the landing ; he had hardly left the water's edge, so anxiously had he been looking for the dear friends who had left him on so perilous, uncertain a venture. And now he helped to bind the ship fast with strong anchor cables, lest a sudden storm might snatch her away, and hastened to give orders to carry ashore the princely cargo.

VII

AT HOME

THEY had not far to go, for King Hygelac, son of Hrethel, had his palace,
where he held court with his peers, within
sight of the sea.   There he dwelt happily
with his Queen, fair Hygd, who, though
she was very young, and had lived but few
winters in her lord's castle, was wise and
of excellent discretion, yet not mean-spir-
ited, nor grudging of gifts to the thanes
and ethelings—very different in all her
ways from another young princess of the
Goths, Thrytho, the moody and the proud,
even to savagery ; so arrogant and fierce
that no man, not even her favourites
among the courtiers, durst look in her
eyes, but he was sure to be taken and

bound by her order, and the knife was quick to follow arrest. Well did nobles and people murmur, and whisper among themselves that such manner was not queenly, nor womanly, for any lady to practise, although peerless of form and feature; for woman should ever be a peace-maker, and not a taker of men's lives—on false pretences too. But no one dared to speak aloud what all thought in their se-cret hearts. So everybody was glad ex-ceedingly when Thrytho was sent off to Angle-land, there to wed the great Offa, King of Mercia, the most powerful of the seven kingdoms. Soon after, however, those who drink at the ale-benches began to tell a different tale, how that she had left off her evil ways from the moment that she reached Offa's hall after her long sea-voyage and been given, gold-adorned, into the noble and brave king's keeping; and ever since, as long as she lived in her royal state, she was famed for her kindness and gentleness; she won and kept the love of that most excellent ruler between the seas—for minstrels tell us that Offa was as famous for his courtly grace and knightly accomplishments as for his feats of war.[1]

Beowulf's arrival was promptly made known to Hygelac. Good news in truth, he thought, that his dear companion, his playfellow of yore, was coming back to him alive and unhurt. Quickly, at his command, the interior of the hall was cleared for the home-coming travellers.

Beowulf sat by the King's side, while his comrades were greeted by their friends, and the gentle Queen moved about the hall with beakers of sweet mead ; for she loved her folk and gladly ministered to them.

With eager, affectionate words Hygelac questioned his kinsman about his voyage, his reception by Hrothgar, the battle for Heorot. Beowulf satisfied him fully on

[1] That these two queens with their contrasting characters were introduced by the Christian writer of the poem to convey a moral lesson, is evident from the allegorical names he gives them : " Hygd," in Anglo-Saxon, means " discretion," and " Thrytho," " haughtiness, superciliousness." At the same time it is not improbable that the name of Thrytho may have been suggested by the actual name of Offa's queen, which was " Cynethryth."

19

all points, and gave him a most detailed account of all that had befallen him, good and evil, during his brief but eventful absence—speaking of his deeds, as was his wont, with heroic simplicity, and dwelling more on Hrothgar's loving-kindness and generosity than upon his own prowess.

When he had told his tale, to which all who were in the hall listened spell-bound, he ordered all Hrothgar's gifts, including four of the beautiful horses, matched to perfection, to be brought into the hall, and then and there presented all to his kinsman and liege lord, bidding him use and enjoy the treasures. As to the carcanet, the curiously wrought, wonderful jewel, which Hrothgar's queen had bestowed on him, he presented that to Queen Hygd, as also three palfreys, keeping only one of the eight horses for his own use, in memory of Hrothgar's friendship. A shining example, truly, of a loyal kinsman's fealty and love, which it were well if all royal kinsmen took to heart. But how many, alack, are there who will, instead, spread the deceitful snare for their trusting comrade's feet and secretly, with wicked guile, contrive his death !

From this time on, Beowulf steadily grew in honours and in his sovereign's confidence. He conducted himself on all occasions wisely and with discretion. Never did he smite his hearth-fellows in their cups. For his was no ruffian soul; but of all mankind he most wisely controlled the great talents which God had given him. Men saw and wondered at him. For they had held him in little esteem for a long time, because of his modest, reserved ways, which did not court attention ; and when he was a lad, he had often been called slack and unpromising. Now, however, every rash judgment was reversed, as the mature man stood radiant in his glory, the very next to the King, who girded him with his own father's gold-mounted battle-sword, King Hrethel's heirloom, than which there was no more renowned weapon among the Goths. At the same time he conferred on him seven thousand hides of land, a princely mansion, and a seat of authority in the Council.

Not many years passed thus peacefully. There was war once more and Hygelac fell in battle in the distant land of the sea-going Frisians. Beowulf saved himself by a feat of swimming which no man but he could have performed, and reached Gothland unharmed. There he found the young widowed Queen, Hygd, beside herself with grief and alarm. She proffered him treasure and realm, jewels and throne; for she had no confidence in her young son Heardred, who was scarcely more than a child, that he would be able to hold the ancestral seats against the Frisians, whose invasion was expected from day to day. But neither she nor the bereaved people could prevail with the loyal kinsman and chieftain to break faith with his dead cousin; he upheld young Heardred in the public assembly, respectfully and with friendly guidance, until the time that he was of full age, when he resigned to him the power which he had wielded only so long as duty bade. But fortune soon after proved fatal to young Heardred. He, too, was killed in war. Then ancient Hrothgar's prophecy came true, and Beowulf found himself King of the Goths. He had not sought or coveted the dignity, giving the elder line always his whole-hearted, undivided service. But when the broad realm came to his hand, he took it as a trust placed in his charge by God, and governed it well for fifty winters, a true ethel-warden —noble guardian of the people. But envious fate, which is ever on the lurk, would not suffer the venerable King to end his days in undisturbed prosperity.

LAY III

THE DRAGON

I

THE TREASURE

IN the land of the Goths, high on a rocky steep above the sea, there stood a lonely stronghold, built of stone. A narrow path led to it from the beach beneath, but it was unfrequented by people, because the castle was tenanted by a Dragon, who had, for three hundred years, kept guard over a treasure of gold and silver—rings, bracelets, jewelled drinking-cups, daggers and swords, and armour of all kinds. This treasure was the legacy of an ancient band of men, war-companions long forgotten. Death took them all off, one after another, and left one solitary survivor, to mourn for lost friends and enjoy for a short while the accumulated wealth.

There was a forsaken barrow on the down near by, where a huge cliff hung sheer over the water. Thither the solitary man carried all the beaten gold and silver, and having buried it all, spoke a few farewell words:

"Hold thou now, O Earth, the wealth of mighty heroes, who cannot guard it any longer. Death in battle has carried them all away, my friends, my peers; they share the bliss of Woden's heavenly hall, where only brave warriors slain in the field are admitted. No one henceforth will furbish the embossed tankard, the precious sword, or the helmet damaskeened with gold; the armour will moulder by the side of the warrior who wore it!"

Thus the sole survivor of a brave company lamented his unhappiness, by day and by night, until the finger of Death touched his heart also, and it stood still.

The dazzling hoard, now unguarded,

was found by the old pest of twilight, that haunteth barrows, the scaly spiteful Dragon, that flieth by night, enwrapt in fire, whom country-folk hold in awe and dread. His great delight is to sit on underground hoards and gloat there. Thus it happened that, having discovered this enormous treasure-house, he held it for three hundred years, until something occurred which angered him and let him loose on the unhappy land.

Some unknown man was fleeing in a feud, houseless and pursued, and in his flight he stumbled on the barrow and on the Dragon asleep therein upon the glittering hoard. Horror-struck, he was turning to escape while he might, but a jewelled tankard caught his eye and he just snatched it before he ran, his heart misgiving him at the time that he was bringing woe on many by the deed. But something impelled him, stronger than reason—so he snatched and ran, hugging the precious bauble, which he carried to his liege lord, who pursued him, as a pledge of peace, and bought his lord's friendship and his own safety therewith. He also revealed the hiding-place of the hoard ; the chieftain hastened thither without delay, the barrow was rifled of many of its jewels, while the Dragon still slept his long, heavy sleep—and the mischief was done !

When the Worm woke and found himself despoiled, his fury was intense ; but he mastered it at first, to make his vengeance more complete and sure. First of all he sniffed at the scent along the rock, and at once came upon the track of the enemy, whose foot had stepped unawares by his very head as he lay asleep. He sought diligently for the man, going over the ground whither the scent took him ; in more and more fiery and raging mood he kept swinging around and around the barrow. There was not any man there in all that desert waste. All the while he matured in his breast his purpose of dire and bloody work. Every now and then he would dash back into the barrow, as though to satisfy himself once more of what he knew already : that there had been plunder done,—then he would dash out again. He could hardly wait for the night to come. But presently the day waned at last, and the Worm had his will : no longer would he bide in fenced walls, but issue forth, equipped with fire, to do havoc all over the land. Thus it was that the Dragon's vengeance had a sore beginning for the people ; soon it was to have a sorer ending for their ruler and benefactor.

II

THE ATTACK

ONCE the monster had begun his fiery raids, he did not stop them again. Far into each night blazed the farmsteads, late so cheerful. The flying pest would fain have left nothing alive where his vast form hovered in the air on broad black pinions, like to a huge smoke-cloud, with live-coal eyes and flame squirting and snorting from open maw and distended nostrils. It was only just before the break of day that he shot back again to his dark mansion for protection; for he trusted his rocky keep; only that trust deceived him in the end.

Soon it was reported to Beowulf (for evil tidings travel swift and sure), that his own mansion, noblest of buildings, even his own royal seat, the gift of the Goths, was melting away in fiery waves. So sorely was the venerable King smitten to the heart at this great outrage, that he was tempted to break out into revilings against Providence, much against his wont, for never was man gentler in his valour, more pious in his power.

Deeply did Beowulf revolve in his thoughts how he should deliver himself and his people from this new pest, after the many, many years of peace and happiness. The memories of his youth, of the time when he, a victorious boy, had purged Hrothgar's hall, single-handed, of Grendel and his loathsome brood, were still green with him, and the thought of going forth to seek the Dragon with a host, or even a band of men, was abhorrent to him. He decided to go and look about him with only eleven companions, led by the finder of the first jewelled tankard, the cause of the baleful feud, who went as the thirteenth of the party. Then the aged King sat him down on the headland, and began to bid farewell to his hearth-fellows. For his heart was heavy within him and full of boding sadness, and his thoughts travelled back, as aged men's thoughts are apt to do when they feel the hour of the last separation drawing nigh—back across the entire field of life's achievements, dwelling longest on what looms remotest. Thus now the ancient warrior, while going over the days of his youth in rather rambling speech, dwelt most lovingly on the time when, as a stripling, he did page's service at the court of Hygelac's father, Hrethel, to whom his own father gave him when only seven years old, and who had raised and fostered him, and held him as dear as his own sons. Then, turning back to the present and its stern necessities, he addressed an affectionate word to each of his more familiar comrades, still harping on his dislike to fight the monster with any but naked hands :

" I would not willingly bear sword or weapon to meet this Worm, as I formerly did not against Grendel. I expect to meet scorching fire, deadly venom ; therefore shall I carry a strong shield and wear a fine mail-shirt. As for you, my men-at-arms, wait ye here on the mountain to see which of us twain falls, deadly stricken there on the rock."

As he spoke, the brave old warrior rose by the brink of the down and sternly scanned the place around, when, not far from where they stood, he beheld a rocky arch, and out of it a stream breaking from the barrow, steaming hot, so no man might come nigh the hoard unscorched and survive the Dragon's flame.

Then did the Prince of the Goths let forth out of his breast a mighty battle-shout, which stirred the keeper of the hoard under his hoary rock. There was now no time for reflection or for parley-ing, for from out the rock there came the hot reeking breath of the monster, like a cloud of steam; and hardly had the hero swung his shield and taken his stand well up by it, when the ringy Worm suddenly rolled forth and buckled himself into a bow, and thus, curved like an arch, emit-ting flame, advanced upon his human foe in a rapid, gliding shuffle. The shield, indeed, protected awhile the glorious chieftain, but when he raised his arm to smite with the sword, which he had been persuaded to take, the stroke, though hard, proved inefficient, and only roused the furious Dragon to greater rage, so that now it cast forth devouring fire in volumes and the deadly sparks sprang every way.

And now, when the combatants closed again, the monster's breast shot steam in scalding jets, and the man stood at bay, unseen for the fire which encompassed him. And of his own band of eleven comrades, sons of ethelings all, not one stood his ground, but all, horror stricken, slunk away to the woods for shelter.

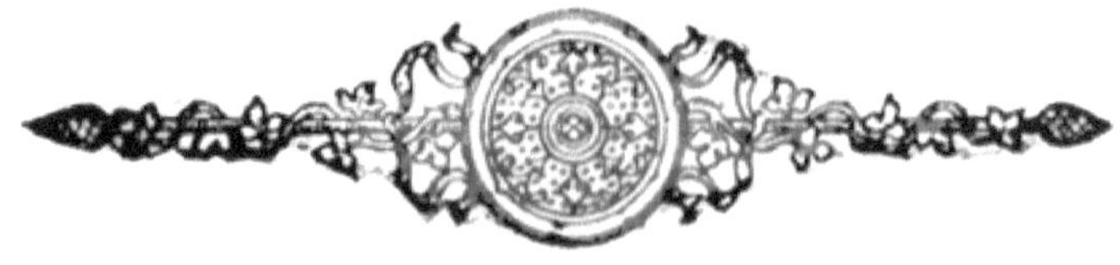

III

WIGLAF

NO, not all. One among them proved a faithful follower,—Wiglaf, Weohstan's son, Beowulf's youngest comrade and his much-loved kinsman. When he beheld his liege lord in such sore distress, his heart smote him, as he thought of the lands and honours the King had so lately bestowed on him, and of the justice he had publicly rendered him and his father in a just feud—and gratitude moved him deeply.

This was the first adventure on which the young etheling had embarked with his liege lord. When he saw his fellows shamefully scurrying off, mindful only of their own safety, he turned on them and upbraided them with hottest words of noble anger.

"What!" he cried, "and shall we thus forsake our lord, with whom we were fain to revel in the festive hall, drinking his mead, taking his golden rings and well-tempered swords? He chose us out of all his host for this adventure because he counted us stout warriors and loyal friends. Now the day is come when he needs the strength of his followers. No matter that he intended to achieve this great deed single-handed—let us stand by him! God knows that I for one had liefer the flame would swallow me up with him than stand away now! I think it shame that we should bear our shields safe home unless we rescue the life of our lord. Is this acting according to our old customs, that we leave him, alone of noble Goths, to bear the brunt and fall in an unequal fight?"

Thus speaking, young Wiglaf boldly plunged into steam and smoke, with his helmet on his head, shouting loud:

"My liege Beowulf! now make good the boast of thy youth, that never in thy lifetime wouldst thou suffer thy glory to decline,—and I shall stand by thee and support thee to the uttermost."

The fell, malignant monster heard the cheering words and came on with redoubled fury, to engage his hated enemies. In an instant the wooden lining of Wiglaf's shield was consumed by the flame; but he went forward under shelter of his elder kinsman's shield when his own was reduced to ashes. Then the old fire of battle burned high in the valiant King's breast, and he smote the Worm so desperate a blow, that the weapon stood in his head, deep stuck; but Naegling, the good sword, flew in splinters as it struck, betraying its master as other blades had done before; for it was not given him that steel should help him in a fight.

And now, enraged even unto death, the Dragon, after yielding ground somewhat, made a rush at the hero, whose strength was giving way apace, and, opening wide his reeking jaws, enclosed his foe's neck with his sharp, long fangs, till the blood flowed in streams.

IV

VICTORY AND DEATH

LOUD is the minstrels' song in praise of Wiglaf, the fearless young etheling, and the prowess he displayed in his aged kinsman's behalf, giving him time to recover his senses, so that at the monster's third onslaught, he could draw the knife from his belt and gash the Worm from below, in the middle, with deadly stab. This was the supreme hour of triumph in the hero's career, when his winged, scaly foe fell off writhing and gasping out his life.

But in the wound which those cruel fangs had inflicted, the venom began its deadly work. In vain young Wiglaf, sitting down on a stone by the mound where his liege lord lay exhausted, applied all the remedies taught him by the leech-lore of cunning dwarfs,—unloosened the helmet, cooled the swelling neck with water which he ladled on it with his hand, and laid on healing herbs which grew in plenty out of the bountiful earth : the hurt was mortal, with each moment life was burning away, with the fiery poison spreading through all the vital parts. Beowulf knew that the tale of his days was told, and he was spending his last hours on earth. But the hero's brave soul did not quail. He looked death in the face, now that it bent close over him, as calmly as he was wont in the days when it was but a distant shadow on the battle-field. The one regret which he expressed was at having no son to whom he could bequeath his royal armour. But he took comfort in the consciousness of having been a just ruler.

"I have ruled this people fifty winters," he said ; "there was not a king who dared threaten them with war. Yet did I hold my own by justice. I have not sought unjust quarrels nor have I sworn many false oaths. Thinking of all this, I am able, though sick unto death with many wounds, to take comfort, for the Ruler of men cannot charge me with murder of kinsmen, when my life quitteth the body."

Yet the dying hero had one wish which he begged his young kinsman to satisfy ere his sight and senses failed him ; he fain would have a glimpse of the treasure which he had bought with his life : " Now quickly go thou, beloved Wiglaf," he said to his faithful comrade, "and examine the treasure under the hoary rock, now the Worm lieth dead. I would have a look at the curious gems, the hoarded store ; then would I more contentedly resign my life and the lordship I have held so long."

Not a moment did the devoted youth lose in obeying his beloved lord's behest. He hurried to the lair of the Worm and gazed with amazement on the numberless and wondrous things of value which filled the barrow, heaped and crushed together, indenting the ground where the Dragon had lain on them. The gold was losing its burnish, the precious stones were fall-ing out, bracelets and helmets were eaten

by rust, losing their value day by day.
Thus can treasure, buried idly in the
earth, make fools of men ! One great
marvel of cunningest handicraft Wiglaf
beheld looming high above the hoard ; it
was a banner, all golden, which gave forth
a gleam of light so bright that it illumined
the darkest recesses of the hollow barrow
and made it easy to examine all the hidden curiosities.

In great haste, hardly pausing to glance
at the uncovered treasure, Wiglaf gathered into his bosom and arms cups and
platters, bracelets and rings, and snatch-
ing also the magic banner, eagerly returned to the mound with his spoils,
anxiously wondering in his faithful heart
whether he should find his lord alive still
where he left him painfully breathing.
Dropping the riches on the ground without a thought of them, he quickly knelt by
the side of his King, and again began to
sprinkle him with water, till he had restored him to consciousness and speech.
As Beowulf opened his eyes and beheld
the gold for a glimpse of which he had

longed, his brow cleared, and he spoke in feeble, but cheerful tones:

"I do give thanks to the Lord of all, the Giver of all things, for those spoils upon which I here do gaze; to think that I have been permitted to acquire such great wealth for my earls and thanes to enjoy and to remember me by after my death! I have sold my life for this treasure—do thou now provide for my men, for I shall be with them no more. Order my brave warriors to erect a lofty cairn— a mound of stones, after the death-fire has burned out, here on the headland above the sea. It shall tower aloft for a memorial to my friends, and seafaring men shall call it Beowulf's Barrow, as they drive their foamy barks over the dangerous waters."

Then the dying hero took off his gold collar and with feeble hands gave it to the young thane; also bade him take his coroneted helmet and his mail-shirt, and wear them and do honour to his chieftain's armour.

Once more the King spoke, with failing

breath : " Thou art the last remnant of
our race.   " Fate has swept all my kinsmen into eternity, princes in chivalry ; and
now I must follow them."

This was the aged monarch's last speech ;
with the words his soul fled from his bosom,
to enter into the everlasting rest of the
righteous.

V

WIGLAF'S REBUKE—DISMAY AND TEARS

A SAD, agonizing hour it was for the warm-hearted youth, new to the world and its trials, when he sat upon the ground taking in the first great grief of his life, as he gazed on the body of the man who had been dearest to him on earth. Small comfort he took from the sight of his dead foe, the horrible Dragon, as he lay at a little distance, uncoiled and harmless for evermore. Weary of heart, but still nursing some sort of stubborn, unavailing hope, he sat by his lord's shoulder and still kept sprinkling him with water, till he saw his ten faint-hearted comrades, as they came sneaking shamefacedly from the woods, slowly trailing their shields along to the place where the King lay dead.

Grief gave way to righteous anger at the sight. Sternly did young Wiglaf look upon the men he no longer loved, and bitter rebuke flowed unchecked from his lips.

" Now, look you," he cried ; " well may a man who is minded to speak the truth, say that the chieftain who gave you those costly gewgaws, that warlike apparel in which you stand there before me, who at the ale-bench so often presented his thanes with helmet and mail-shirt, utterly and wretchedly threw his gifts away. For, verily, little cause had he to boast of his companions-in-arms in the hour of danger ! Nevertheless, it was given him by God, the Ordainer of victories, to avenge himself single-handed when his valour was put to the proof. For little protection could I afford him, though I attempted what was beyond my strength, in trying to help my kinsman. Now go, ye cravens ! No share of the treasure is there for you or yours. And may every man of your kin be sent forth into life-long exile, deprived of lands and rights, as soon as the ethelings now at a distance come together and are told of your disloyalty, your shameful desertion. Go—and learn from experience that, to a warrior, death is better far than a life of shame!"

When he had relieved his feelings by this thundering outburst, Wiglaf gave orders to make the woful issue of the conflict known to the host of thanes and earls who, by the master's command, had been encamped over the sea-cliff and had sat there all day long by their shields, their souls divided betwixt hope and fear. One young thane rode up the bluff, sent by the rest, to view the fatal scene and report to them, which he did faithfully, in words pregnant with grief for the present and foreboding for the near future.

"Now we may soon look for war," he concluded his report; "as soon as the King's death is made known among the Franks and Frisians. For never, since Hygelac fell, have we enjoyed the good-will of the Merovingian Kings of the Franks, nor do I count upon peace or good understanding on the side of the Swedes—such is the feud and grudge of

all these nations ever since the fall of
Hygelac on Frisian land. They will surely
attack us as soon as they learn that our
Prince is dead, he who has so long upheld
against all foes our treasure and our realm,
winning ever greater respect in public
counsel, and ever greater fame in war.
Now methinks that quickness were best;
so let us look our last upon the mighty
King, and bring him without delay to the
funeral pyre. And yonder is a hoard of
precious things, gold untold, jewels purchased with our hero's own life-blood.
Never a warrior shall wear any of those
ornaments; never a maiden have on her
neck one of those collars. Sorrowful and
stripped of gold ornaments shall all come
to the funeral procession, while many a
hand shall swing the spear in the cold of
the morning; music of the harp shall not
waken the warriors on the fateful day; but
the ominous raven, fluttering and chatter-
ing of slaughter, will tell the eagle of his
luck, while, alongside of the grim and
hungry wolf, he stripped the slain."

Upon hearing the grief-stricken youth's

discourse, all the troop arose and sadly, under gushing tears, wended their way under the crag, to behold the gruesome sight. There they found, stretched lifeless on the sand, the man who had given them so many rings in bygone times, and, at but a short distance from him, the carcase of the loathsome beast, all scorched with its own flames—never saw they more frightful object. It was fifty feet long where it lay. No more through the regions of air would he sportively whirl at midnight, then down again pounce to rejoice in his lair—he would have no use for caverns any more. And there, unwatched, open to all men's eyes, lay bowls and dishes and swords of price, all rusty and corroded, as though they had lain in the earth's lap a thousand winters ; for this treasure had been bound by a magic spell, so that it might never be touched of man, unless God Himself granted to one of His choice to open the enchanted hoard ; and that man was to leave his life as ransom— such was Beowulf's lot.

VI

THE OBSEQUIES

AND now Wiglaf once more lifted up his voice :

" Alas ! we were not able to convince our beloved master that he should not challenge yonder monster, but should leave him to dwell unmolested in his haunts to the end of the world. But it is done—the hoard lies open before us, purchased at a fearful price. I was inside the chamber of the barrow and explored the whole of it, and all the stores it held ; for, once the price was paid, the spell was broken, and the passage open to all. Hurriedly I grabbed with my hands a huge burden of treasure and carried it hither to the feet of my King. He was still alive then, wise and sensible ; freely did he talk, although the death-pang was upon him. And he bade me give you all his greeting and tell you his will : that ye should build up, in memory of your chieftain's deeds, on the very place of the funeral pyre, a stone-cairn of the highest, forasmuch as he was of all men the most famous warrior, as long as it was given him to dwell in his royal castle. And now let us go, all together, and visit the fatal hoard. I will be your guide, and ye shall have your fill of gazing on gold and jewels. After that, let us make ready the bier, and promptly equip it, and so let us convey our beloved master to the place where he shall tarry long in the keeping of the Almighty."

Then, by Wiglaf's orders, commands were sent round to many householders, that they should haul timber, stout and sound, to do the last service to the ruler of men.

While this was being done, Wiglaf called out of the band seven of the King's thanes, the choicest ; led by him, the eighth, they went under the dangerous roof, one warrior walking in front, bearing in his hand a flaming torch. When they had taken a view of the treasure, lying there keeperless and undefended, they did not stand upon the order of casting lots as to who should loot the hoard, but went to work with all despatch to empty the chamber. Then, taking hold of the dead Dragon, they haled him away and shoved him over the precipitous cliff. With a great splash the waves engulfed him, and that was the last of him. In the meantime, the gold was laden on waggons, which followed the bier whereon the hero was borne to the high, jutting headland which he had chosen for his resting-place.

There they constructed for him a huge pyre, which they hung all round with helmets, battle-shields, bright mail-shirts ; and in the midst of the pyre, heaving deep sighs, they laid their beloved lord. Then the warriors set fire to the pile in several places ; the smoke, heavy and black, mounted up to the sky, the ruddy flames shot aloft, their roaring mingling with the howling of the winds, until the house of flesh and bone was utterly consumed.

With sore hearts and care-laden minds, the warriors stood around and silently mourned their liege lord, the while a dirge of sorrow was sung by an aged dame, whose dishevelled hair streamed in the wind. The blue heavens swallowed up the black smoke.

Then did the people go to work and construct a barrow and a cairn of stones on the hill. It was high and broad, and sea-faring men would behold it from a great distance. Ten days they laboured. With great skill they surrounded the ashes of the pyre with a noble embankment, and the pile rose like a beacon for all coming ages, even as the memory of the hero's deeds and noble character.

As to the fated hoard, they buried the whole in the barrow under the cairn, and left it there, where it remains to this day as useless to mankind as it has been ever since the last of a company of unknown earls consigned it to the earth's keeping.

Last of all funeral ceremonies, twelve youths, sons of ethelings, rode around the barrow. From time to time they stopped in the race, to bewail their loss, and bemoan their King, to recite an elegy in his honour, to celebrate his name and rehearse his deeds, extolling his manhood with admiring words.

Thus did the nobles of the Goths, the companions of his hearth, lament the fall of Beowulf, their lord. They said that he was of all kings in the world the mildest and most affable to his men, most genial to his nobles, and most desirous of glory.

NOTE ON THE "BEOWULF"

NO monument of ancient national literature has been—and to a great extent still is—so overlooked and underrated
as the Anglo-Saxon epic of " Beowulf." It
has, indeed, been edited and re-edited, and
duly commented on, and it is entered in
the university curriculum of Anglo-Saxon.
But how great a proportion of even interested students pursue their English studies
as far back as Anglo-Saxon ? A cultured
general reader would vainly ask for a
readable translation, even in prose, of the
" Beowulf ;" nor would he be likely to
ask for one, as there is nothing in even
the best histories of English literature,
native or foreign, to awaken a feeling
of sympathetic curiosity—nothing more
than either a bare mention, or at best,
a brief account, always insufficient and fre-

quently misleading.   And—proof positive
of the poem's total lack of popularity—it
has never yet been illustrated.

An untoward fate seemed to pursue the
" Beowulf" even before it came into the
hands of the scholars.   There is only one
manuscript of it in existence, which is hid
away among nine others, comparatively
unimportant, in a folio volume labelled
Vitellius A, XV., and belonging to the
Cottonian Library in the British Museum.
It was noticed for the first time, in 1705,
in a catalogue of Anglo-Saxon manuscripts
(Wanley's), in which it is described as
containing an account of certain wars
between Sweden and Denmark.   Need-
less to say it is nothing of the kind.   The
notice was not inviting, and nobody paid
much attention to it.   One hundred years
later, in 1807, Sharon Turner mentioned
the poem in his *History of the Anglo-
Saxons*, and even attempted a translation
of a few extracts, with but indifferent
success, owing to the then still very imper-
fect knowledge of Anglo-Saxon versifica-
tion and poetic language.   Still, the poem

was now treated with respect, and the study of it was taken up conscientiously, by some even enthusiastically.

But the students encountered difficulties which they would have been spared a hundred or even eighty years before : the original manuscript—the only one—was no longer intact. It had been badly injured in a fire which broke out in the Cottonian Library in 1731, destroying 114 volumes and damaging 98 others, "so as to make them defective," in the words of the report ; and among these "defective" ones was our folio. Numerous leaves were scorched, and of these, again, many chipped off in the course of time, doing away with many ends of lines. The loss, of course, is irretrievable, but fortunately not so great as to impair materially the sense and the value of the whole. Strangely enough, the same fate, only worse, overtook the first attempt at an edition of the poem. The Danish scholar, Thorkelin, had brought home two complete copies of it, for purposes of study and translation. During twenty years he gave the work much time, off and on, and had the poem almost ready for the press when, in 1807, his house was burned down during the bombardment of Copenhagen by the English, and his edition of the " Beowulf " perished, with most of his books However, the two manuscript copies having fortunately escaped destruction, Thorkelin had the extraordinary courage to do the work over again, and in 1815 came out the first edition of the " Beowulf,"—the first printed text, with a parallel Latin translation and indices.   Since then scholars have done their duty by this noble monument— in every way except making it popular.

Coming now to the discussion of the poem itself, the peculiarity which strikes us most at the first reading is that, while it is avowedly the national epic of the Anglo-Saxons and one of the oldest monuments of the Anglo-Saxon language, the hero is a Goth, and the action takes place

---

[1] A very complete survey of the critical and philological work done on the " Beowulf " up to date will be found in the Introduction to Professor John Earle's literal prose translation (with notes) published at Oxford in 1892.

in Denmark and in Sweden. Yet the scenery described is that of a part of Northumbria, in England, which can be identified to this day, and some of the names of the locality are said to tally with those in the poem. It would seem, therefore, that the Angles and Saxons, who were near neighbours of the Danes in the German mother-country, brought the story over to the British Island and it was retold in literary poetic form before the Danes came over as pirates and conquerors. Had the poem been written after this event, a Swedo-Danish hero could hardly have been adopted by the subjugated Anglo-Saxons, nor could the Danes have been mentioned with such absolute absence of animosity.

Another not only peculiar but highly puzzling feature is that there are two Beowulfs : the second king of the Skylding dynasty (also called Beow), Beowulf the Dane ; and the hero of the poem, Beowulf the Goth, who comes over the sea, with a picked band of Goths, to deliver the Skyldings from a most untoward visitation.

What makes this thing stranger still, is that the poem begins with a glorification of the warlike Danes, leading us to expect that it is their national hero whose exploits we are to be called upon to admire. Instead of which, the Danes appear only in the not very admirable *rôle* of people who endure an intolerable nuisance passively for twelve years, unable to rid themselves of it—a fact which is duly brought home to them by their deliverer in a moment of legitimate irritation. The reason for this curious incongruity lies almost certainly in the alterations which the old story underwent,—as all epic stories did in the progress of oral transmission, and even in the first written attempts, which were often cast and re-cast before they reached their final form. Originally, the second Beowulf was certainly a Dane and a Skylding. As such, he would quite naturally and properly be named after the ancestor who is held up as a model prince in the prologue. The latest criticism detects in the poem itself traces amounting to intrinsic proof that such was the case. It was natural that Beowulf, himself a Skylding, should be the champion and deliverer of his people and house, and, after the death of the aged king, should be called to the throne by the country for which he had laboured and fought.   Gothland is evidently, to use the clever French phrase, "dragged in by the hair"; by whom and for what reason, is immaterial to the mere reading of the story,   But a genealogical connection between the two Beowulfs is felt as an imperious necessity, and the absence of it is a glaring inconsistency which it would be hopeless to attempt to smooth over or explain away for the benefit of youthful readers, whose exacting logic in such things is proverbial.   Wherefore the expedient has been resorted to in the present volume of making the second Beowulf a Skylding *by his mother*—an expedient innocent enough, since we are not told who was his mother; and why could not a royal daughter of Denmark be married to a royal thane of Gothland ?

As to the authorship of the poem, it is of course obscure. But the latest criticism shows good reason to ascribe it to a high Church dignitary—possibly Hygeberht, Bishop of Litchfield—statesman and courtier at the time of the great Offa II., King of Mercia (mentioned with great, but not servile praise in Lay II.), who in the second half of the eighth century gathered the entire Heptarchy under his overlordship. The few historical touches betray the man versed in the affairs of more countries than his own.[1]

[1] For the very interesting development of this hypothesis, as well as for other points of exhaustive research and criticism, see J. Earle's Introduction, already alluded to.

Professor Earle's version has been fully utilised in the present volume, even to the extent of frequently making use of its wording, where it was not too archaic or literal for ordinary reading purposes.

KEY TO THE PRONUNCIATION OF PROPER NAMES.

Aeschere . . .	Es'-kâ-râ.
Alberich . . .	Äl'-ber-ic.
Balmung . . .	Bäll'-mung.
Bechlaren . . .	Bec-lä'-ren.
Beowulf . . .	Bï'-o-wulf.
Breca	Brâ'-kä.
Brunhilde . . .	Brun-hil'-dâ.
Dankwart . . .	Dank'-värt.
Eckewart . . .	Eck'-e-värt.
Etzel	Et'-sel.
Folker . . .	Foll'-ker.
Gernot . . .	Gêr'-nŏt.
Giselher . . .	Gï'-zel-hâr.
Grendel . . .	Gren'-del.
Gunther . . .	Gun'-ter.
Hagen . . .	Häg'-en.
Hela	Hâ'-lä.
Helferich . . .	Hel'-fer-ic.
Helke . . .	Hel'-kâ
Heorot . . .	Hï'-o-rŏt.
Heremod . . .	Hâ'-re-mŏd.
Hildebrand . .	Hil'-de-bränd.

* Hrethel . . .	Hrä'-thel.
* Hrothgar . . .	Hroth'-gar.
* Hrunting . . .	Hrunt'-ing.
Hygd	Hïgd.
Hygeberht . . .	Hig'-e-bêrt.
Hygelac . . .	Hig'-e-läc.
Isenstein . . .	Ï'-sen-stīne.
Kriemhilde . .	Krïm-hil'-dâ.
Ludegast . . .	Lū'-de-gäst.
Naegling . . .	Nâg'-ling.
Nibelungs . .	Nï'-be-lungs.
Ortewein . . .	Orr'-te-vīne.
Rudiger . . .	Rū'-di-ger.
Siegfried . . .	Sïg'-frïd.
Sieglinde . . .	Sïg-lin'-dâ.
Siegmund . . .	Sïg'-mund.
Skyldings . . .	Skïld'-ings.
Thrytho . . .	Thrï'-thō.
Tronje . . .	Tron'-yâ.
Unferth . . .	Un'-ferth.
Ute	U'-tâ.
Valkyrie . . .	Väl-kïr'-yâ.
Wealhtheow . .	Wel'-thē-ō.
Weohstan . . .	Wï'-ō-stan.
Wiglaf . . .	Wig'-läf.
Wolfhart . . .	Volf'-härt.
Worms . . .	Vorrms.
Wulfgar . . .	Wulf'-gär.
Xante . . .	Kzän'-tâ.

* The H to be aspirated.

9 783337 213961